The Legend of Little Man Wolf

Gilbert M. De Los Reyes

Order this book online at www.trafford.com/08-1061
or email orders@trafford.com

Most Trafford titles are also available at major online book retailers.

Note for Librarians: A cataloguing record for this book is available from Library and Archives Canada at www.collectionscanada.ca/amicus/index-e.html

ISBN: 978-1-4251-8555-8

We at Trafford believe that it is the responsibility of us all, as both individuals and corporations, to make choices that are environmentally and socially sound. You, in turn, are supporting this responsible conduct each time you purchase a Trafford book, or make use of our publishing services. To find out how you are helping, please visit www.trafford.com/responsiblepublishing.html

Our mission is to efficiently provide the world's finest, most comprehensive book publishing service, enabling every author to experience success. To find out how to publish your book, your way, and have it available worldwide, visit us online at www.trafford.com/10510

www.trafford.com

North America & international
toll-free: 1 888 232 4444 (USA & Canada)
phone: 250 383 6864 • fax: 250 383 6804
email: info@trafford.com

The United Kingdom & Europe
phone: +44 (0)1865 487 395 • local rate: 0845 230 9601
facsimile: +44 (0)1865 481 507 • email: info.uk@trafford.com

10 9 8 7 6 5 4 3 2

His name was Jeremiah McCall.
He was born to Laughing Deer
of the *Diné* Towering House People clan,
and born for Victor McCall of the Irish People.
The Navajos called him Little Man Wolf.
Just slightly over four feet tall,
he was the fastest, most feared gunfighter who ever lived.

CHAPTER I

The tall, skinny man at the door leaned over to look out, pushing the swinging door of Betsy's Saloon half-open as he did. The heat from the ground rose up, throwing a sweltering mist in the air. Sweat dripped from the top of his head, down to his forehead, then to his temple.

"What d'ya see out there?" a heavy-set man with a gruff voice asked from where he stood at the bar holding a mug of beer.

"Nothin'. There ain't a thing out there."

The door swung back and forth and made creaking noises as the tall, skinny man let it go. Betsy's Saloon stood directly at the end of the main road. One could stand there by the door and look to see who was coming for miles. Sometimes, when it's late on a hot day like today, the heat rising up from the ground would distort the image, and one had to squint a little to get the sun out of his eyes to see better.

"Are ya sure? He sent word he wuz comin'."

"Jesse, I said there ain't nobody out there but a little farm boy with a dog riding a pinto into town. Maybe he's doing some errand. Finish that beer, and have some whisky. Pour one for me too. You're so goddamned nervous, you're getting on my nerves."

"Maybe you're right, Tom."

"Jesse, that was eight years ago. The boy died in the fire."

"I didn't see a body, did you?"

"No, I didn't have to."

"If he didn't die, he would be a full-grown man of sixteen now."

"He died, okay?" Tom said as he walked back to the bar for his drink.

The man called Jesse was quiet for a while. Then he turned to the bartender and said, "Who was it that said he wuz coming?"

"Man came in this morning as soon as I opened," Wilson, the bartender said. "Says he, Jeremiah McCall wuz comin' fo' ya and Tom."

"What'd he look like?"

"Tall. Mean-lookin' eyes. Carries a gun low on the left side."

"He said his name was Jeremiah McCall?"

"Could be him, but didn't say his name. Just said Jeremiah McCall wuz coming."

"It must be just some mean joke, Jesse. Could be one of our boys putting the scare on us. Don't bother me none."

There was a heavy sound of boots tramping down on the boardwalk outside the saloon, the sound of spurs turning as the boots hit the boards. At first, the sound was faint, then it got louder and louder as it came nearer.

Everybody in the room turned quiet, listening to the sound of the boots. The women held their breath. Jesse moved his right hand slowly up his side, letting it rest on the top of his gun holster. Tom stepped away from the bar and moved closer to the side near the door, kicking a chair as he did.

The swinging door opened slowly. A man slightly over four feet tall walked in. He was wearing a buckskin coat. A tomahawk and a Bowie knife hung at his sides. Two six-shooters were holstered across his chest in a bandoleer. An old dog that looked half wolf stood beside him, head down, eyeing everybody in the room out of the corner of its eyes.

There was a loud sigh of relief in the room followed by laughter, which became boisterous and louder and louder as the people let out their tension.

"Is the circus coming here to Nogales?" Shirley, one of the ladies who sat with the customers asked innocently.

The town had never seen a little man before except in postcards that friends from faraway places sent them.

"I always dreamed of going to the circus one day and seeing those lions and tigers and big elephants," another woman said. "I'm glad they are coming here at last."

"He looks like a little doll with his big wooden toy guns. Look at his nice blonde hair, and very blue eyes," Shirley said.

"Would you sleep with him, Shirley? He's probably a virgin dying for a woman," someone asked with a chuckle.

Shirley had a kind face, and was the prettiest among the ten or so women who worked at the saloon entertaining men from the ranches around and the silver mine up in the hill.

"Sleep with him? I'd suckle him, then hump him until he begs me to stop."

"Ya would too, you bitch!" a man standing at a corner said.

Everybody laughed.

"Son, why don't you move away from the door? We're waiting for someone, and you are in the way," Jesse said.

The laughing stopped. The small man did not say anything. He just stood there, looking intently at the man called Jesse as if he was measuring him.

"My name is Little Man Wolf," the small man said with a deep strong voice.

"Yes, I can see that. You and that old wolf over there are brothers, right?" Jesse said, and everybody laughed.

"Dog's name is Lhachaeh."

"That sounds Injun. What does it mean?"

"Means dog."

"Funny. You Injun?"

"Navajo."

"You have blonde hair and blue eyes. You can't be Injun."

"Half-breed."

"Half-breed," Jesse repeated the words with a smirk. He hated

Indians.

"That's a Navajo scalp on your belt."

"Yeah. Yeah. Kin of yours?"

"You're Jesse Fremont."

"Yes, why?"

"And you, Tom Baxter?" Little Man Wolf asked the man standing on the side. Tom nodded, beginning to be apprehensive.

The dog started growling at the man.

"You have a message for us?" Jesse asked.

Little Man Wolf looked at Jesse, studying him.

"I am the message," Little Man Wolf said, unsmiling.

"What d'ya mean, boy?" Tom asked.

"Jeremiah McCall."

"He sent you?" Jesse asked.

There was silence.

"My father called me by that name."

It took Jesse awhile to understand what Little Man Wolf just said. He looked at the two six-shooters strapped across the small man's chest. Then, as if on a signal, Jesse and Tom drew their guns. The guns hardly cleared their holsters when two bullets hit each man dead center in the heart and between the eyes. It happened so quickly the people in the saloon could not believe it. They had seen gunfighters before, but none was as fast as this little man. It was almost as if a flash of lightning had hit the room.

The smell of gunpowder filled the air.

The little man walked slowly over to Jesse's slumped body. He holstered his guns with a quick twirling and twisting of his fingers. Then he pulled out his Bowie knife, cut Jesse's pant belt, and gently slid off the Navajo scalp. Slowly, he tucked it inside his buckskin coat while glaring at each one in the saloon. The dog kept growling by his side. Then, with one quick move, Little Man Wolf grabbed Jesse's head, and slit off his scalp. The women looked away and the men gasped. He walked toward the door, holding the scalp in his hand. Drops of blood fell on the floor. The room was quiet except for the sound of the little man's spurs as his boots hit the wooden surface of the saloon.

The dog made whining sounds and looked up at the little man.

"You waited a long time for this, Lhachaeh. Go ahead," the little man said without looking.

The dog bounded across the room to where Tom Baxter was lying, raised one leg and pissed on the dead man's face.

"You're Jeremiah McCall?" Shirley nervously asked, choking on her words and only half-believing what she had just witnessed.

"Jeremiah died in the fire at the McCall farm eight years ago. Call me Little Man Wolf."

The small man backed up toward the door as the dog looked out toward the street.

"Do not follow. If you step out of the door, Lhachaeh will tear your heart out."

Then he disappeared through the door.

CHAPTER II

"It's a good land," Victor McCall said to Laughing Deer as he led the horses to water in the river. "The soil is fertile. We can plant corn, raise some sheep, and keep a few cattle just for our own needs. Maybe keep a stable of good strong horses to sell to the stagecoach company in town. That town will grow faster than you think. People are coming in every day. They will need provisions and horses. Five miles away is not too far from us, and we can still have peace and quiet over here. Yep, it's a good place to settle in, Laughing Deer."

He paused for a while and looked at his wife. "We are also far away from the troubles of your people up north," he added.

Laughing Deer listened to her husband without looking at him or saying a word.

"Don't worry, your parents will be alright. It was their choice to stay. Colonel Carson had already agreed to let them go with us. They would not have stayed if they thought it was not alright."

Victor unbridled the horses and they walked slowly away to graze.

"Red Lance is a proud warrior," Laughing Deer said softly, as if speaking to herself. "He will not abandon his people, and Weaving Woman will go where he goes. Wrestling Bear is still out there with Chief Manuelito. He can get killed if the soldiers find them."

"Your brother is strong, and can take care of himself."

"He will not surrender. He will fight and get killed."

"Chief Manuelito is wise. He will avoid a fight."

"Chief Manuelito is angry. He will not avoid a fight. He saw what the blue coat soldiers did."

"It was war, Laughing Deer. The Diné, your people, refused to follow the government's order to surrender and move to New Mexico."

She was quiet again. Images of the carnage at Canyon de Chelly up north went through her mind. She could hear the sounds of cannons and gunfire, and the screaming of women and children.

"The blue coats raped our women," she said after awhile.

Victor McCall looked at his wife.

"You saw that happen?"

"Two men grabbed me. They smelled of alcohol and sweat. Jeremiah was there, and he tried to stop them. But he is so little. One man kicked him to the side. I fought, and I screamed."

"You were raped? Oh, God! Why didn't you tell me before?"

"I kept screaming and fighting. Then there was a loud sound of a gun. I was crying and could not see too well. There was a tall man standing there holding a gun pointed at the two men. 'Let her go,' he said. 'Sure, Lieutenant. Just having some fun,' one of the men said. 'If I see you near her again I'll just shoot without asking.' 'Yes, sir Lieutenant!' the other man said."

"What happened afterwards?"

"Nobody bothered us again. But, some of the women came to me later. They said they were raped."

"I'm sorry. Thank God you're alright. What was the name of the Lieutenant?"

"Thomas Murphy, he was called."

"I must remember to thank him when I visit Fort Sumner."

Jeremiah remembered the man. He was tall with dark hair. He had an angry face. After he sent the two men away, he looked at him and his mother. His face was no longer angry, but his eyes were sad. Then he walked away. Jeremiah saw him many times later looking at them from a distance. The soldiers knew he was watching, so no one came near to bother them.

Victor McCall stood up and walked to the river. They did not speak again for a while. Jeremiah followed his father and stood beside him. He was just three years old, and smaller than most boys his age. Victor looked down at his son. Then, he picked up a flat stone and angrily flung it to the water where it skipped three times before it sunk. Jeremiah picked up a stone, too, and threw it to the water where it immediately sunk. They watched the shallow river for a while, listening to the ripples and following them with their eyes as they flowed down and around the pebbles and rocks. After awhile, they walked back slowly to where Laughing Deer was sitting on the ground, and had not moved.

"Bosque Redondo may not be a bad place. The government will see to their needs. They don't have to go hungry," Victor McCall said.

"How many promises have they kept? How many treaties has the government broken with the Navajo? What have they done to the Apache and the Cherokee? You are my husband Victor, and you are wise in many ways. Your heart is true, and I want to believe you. But I don't believe your government. And now, there is the war between your people in the north and south. They are killing each other. If they can kill each other, what will stop them from killing us?"

"Let's not think about that anymore. We have things to do now. We will build a proper house for you and Jeremiah on this land. But, for now, we will build a hogan right here, close to the river so you don't have to walk too far to fetch the water."

"The hogan is all the house we need," Laughing Deer said.

Victor McCall did not hear what his wife said. He was preoccupied with what had happened and the things he had to do.

Nothing was said anymore about Red Lance and Weaving Woman, or of Bosque Redondo. They started gathering the materials they needed for the hogan without saying a word. Victor McCall felled a tree for suitable logs, while Laughing Deer stripped bark and gathered long poles. By mid afternoon they had all they needed for the hogan.

"We start building tomorrow at dawn so we can finish before nightfall," Victor McCall said.

"You learned well," Laughing Deer said, now smiling.

"Red Lance taught me well. He said you must build a hogan in one day. If not finished by nightfall, the evil ones will come and possess it and cause illnesses."

Laughing Deer looked at the sky and sniffed the air. Springtime is the perfect time to build a hogan. It is the time to renew the spirit, mind and body. It is the time to plant new seeds for the crop. She looked toward the northeast where Diné Land was. They had traveled too far south, away from her homeland. The thought gave her a feeling of apprehension, which she could not understand. There was no more reason to be afraid, she thought. She and Jeremiah were now safe with her husband. The troubles up north were behind them. Victor was right. This was a good piece of land to settle in.

"It's time start a fire. It will be cold and dark soon," she said standing up to gather wood and prepare supper.

Victor called the horses in with a whistle, and they came running. Then he started to tether their legs to a tree so they would not wander about in the night.

After supper, Laughing Deer prepared the blanket for Jeremiah to sleep on.

"You must sleep now," she said, "so you will wake up early. The Holy People travel at Dawn. They will only bless those who wake up early."

"Will they bless you too?" Jeremiah asked.

"Yes, if I wake up early."

"And father too?"

"Yes. He will be up early." Then to Victor, "If one sleeps too much, he will grow old early, and his skin will be wrinkled."

Just then a coyote howled in the night.

"Now, what is that trickster coyote up to this time?" Victor McCall said, for the benefit of his wife. The coyote was noted for playing tricks on the Diné, according to the Navajo legend.

Laughing Deer smiled. Yes, Red Lance had taught him well.

Victor McCall was up before dawn. He immediately laid out the floor plan for the hogan, exactly the way Red Lance had shown him. 'This is the way Talking God taught my people long, long ago,' Red Lance had said. 'This is the sacred way. You must build hogan the way Talking God said to get full blessing.'

The entrance faced northeast toward Diné Land. The four posts represented the four sacred Navajo mountains that marked the boundaries of their territory. By the time Laughing Deer and Jeremiah were up, Victor McCall already had the poles securely sunk in the ground.

"My husband does not want to grow old quickly and have wrinkled skin," Laughing Deer said, teasing. "You were up too early. But, now you eat first so you will have more strength."

Jeremiah was still sleepy, but he was up.

"Did the Holy People come?" he asked.

"They did, and they already blessed you when they saw you waking up. Now, eat."

They started working as soon as they finished eating. By late morning, Victor was finished with the sides of the hogan, and started working on the domed roof. Laughing Deer and Jeremiah worked on the bark and packed the earth all around the sides. Before sunset, the hogan was finished. They all looked at their work and felt satisfied.

"We have no shaman to bless the hogan," Laughing Deer said sadly. "But we must perform the Blessing Way ceremony ourselves to honor Changing Woman and obtain peace, harmony, protection, a long and happy life, and to be at one with the universe, with Mother Earth and Father Sky."

"Then we must," Victor agreed.

At the middle of the hogan, Laughing Deer started a fire with aromatic cedar wood. The sweet smell from the burning wood filled the air. Then they sat around the fire.

"I do not know the chant," Victor McCall said.

"I know you do not know the song, my husband."

"Yes, I meant the song. I never really learned the song."

"Just sit quietly and listen," she said to Victor and Jeremiah.

Then, she started singing the Blessing Way song.

CHAPTER III

It took awhile to get established and sink the roots in, but everything seemed to be working out as Victor McCall had envisioned. The town grew fast and businesses were established. The miners came, and soon saloons and all kinds of entertainment were all over the place.

The McCall farm now had a fine log cabin, a barn with horse stalls, an outside corral with mustangs that still had to be broken in, and a herd of sheep. The field was planted with corn, which grew tall and healthy, promising good yields every year.

Since Victor made regular trips to town to buy supplies or to deliver sheep to the butcher shop, he had made friends with some good folks over there. Everybody seemed to know them by now. Once in awhile, some nice people from the town would come and visit. At first, Laughing Deer was apprehensive in close contact with the white people, but some church ladies who sincerely meant well made her feel more comfortable. However, for the most part, the McCall's kept to themselves.

On one of the trips to town where Jeremiah accompanied his father, they went to see Doctor Kraus. He was a nice old man who took care of everybody in town. Jeremiah overheard the doctor saying something about him to his father.

"I would not say the condition is normal, Victor. I am saying the occurrence is not unusual. This is an inherited disorder in bone or cartilage development. The body parts will tend to grow disproportionately. Do you have any member of your family with the same condition?"

"No, nobody comes to mind."

"Any grandparents or ancestor you can think of?"

"No."

"This is a common occurrence in Europe. It can happen to the best people. Don Sebastian de Morra of the royal court of Spain was a short man. Sir Jeffrey Hudson, 17th century royalty and a very handsome person, looked like a child. Even the Talmud mentions that the second son of the Egyptian Pharaoh was short of stature."

"Is there anything than can be done?"

"Unfortunately, the science of medicine has not yet advanced to such a level that it could undo what God made and has given you. I'm sorry, Victor."

"What will happen to him?"

"Fortunately, the child is healthy. From what I can see, all parts of his body are normal, except his legs. They will lag behind in growth."

"Which means?"

"He will not grow as tall as you."

"What will happen to him then?" Victor said again, as if he was talking to himself.

"Victor. God is not an evil god. He makes all of us a certain way to fulfill a certain purpose. Whatever that purpose is, only God himself knows. But, he will lead the way for us to discover it for ourselves. He challenges us to make ourselves better. He may take away something, but He will give something else to equip us better for his challenge. People with a condition like your son's learn to adjust, compensate, and even outdo themselves. Keep faith, Victor. Trust God."

They were quiet on the way back. Several times, Victor looked at Jeremiah as if he wanted to say something to him. But, he did not say anything. As they neared home, Victor put his arms around his son. Jeremiah thought he heard his father say softly, "I'm sorry son." Jeremiah understood what the doctor said about his condition. But, he did not let on that he heard.

Jeremiah spent his days by himself most of the time. After he had done his chores and helped tend the sheep, he would be out in the field chasing butterflies, playing with tadpoles, or scaring dragonflies. Once in a while, he would sneak into the hogan, which they had kept where it always stood, even after his father had built the large log cabin beside it. He found the hogan gave him a feeling far different from what he felt when he was in the log cabin. His mother had decorated the hogan with all kinds of Navajo trinkets. There were paintings of the sun and the moon in the sky, and a leather pouch with herbs, blue turquoise, white shell, jet-black stone, and yellow abalone shell. When he could not find his mother at home, he knew she would be in the hogan. He would join her there and just sit quietly beside her. Sometimes Laughing Deer would be singing a Navajo song softly to herself.

"Mother, what were you singing?" Jeremiah asked her one day after she finished.

"It was a prayer for the safety of Red Lance, Weaving Woman, and Wrestling Bear."

"Do you miss them?"

"Yes."

"I can't remember what they look like."

"You were still very little. You will remember when you see them again."

"When will I see them again?"

"Soon."

Just then, they heard a wagon drive in.

"Your father is home. Go, run and greet him."

Jeremiah ran to greet his father. He was truly happy to see him after a whole day of absence. But, he was also anxious to see what he brought back for them from the town.

"Where is your mother?"

"In the hogan."

"Quick! Call her, then come back inside the house."

"What is it?" Laughing Deer asked when she came in and saw Victor with his rifle looking out the window.

"Lock the back door and close all the windows. Then get yourself a rifle."

"What is it Victor?"

"Some Indians are coming our way. Not Navajo."

Laughing Deer quickly locked the back door, closed all the windows, and then peeped through the gun port, ready to shoot.

Victor was right, she thought. They were not Navajo. Neither were they Hopi or Apache.

The ten warriors lined up in front of the house as soon as they arrived, clearly exposing themselves to any shooter inside. They just sat there on their horses for a long time without doing anything. Finally, the headman called out. Victor did not say anything. He just watched through the gun port in the window. The headman called out again.

"Victor, I can understand a few words he is saying. It sounds like Apache, but he is not Apache."

"What is he saying?"

"I think he says, he only wants to talk?"

"Tell him to say what he wants."

Laughing Deer spoke to the headman in the Apache language, and the headman gave a lengthy response, complete with sign language, pointing to the sky and the earth.

"What did he say?"

"He said he knows I am Navajo, and we have a little boy with golden hair. He saw us when we first came three years ago. He saw us build the hogan, and heard me sing the Blessing Way song. Navajo like to lodge in hogans, not teepees, he said. That is how he knew I am Navajo."

The headman spoke again.

"What is he saying now?"

"He says his people are not at war with Navajo. They mean us no harm. He just wants to talk, but he wants to see your eyes so he knows you understand why they are here."

"Fine. Tell him I am coming out, but I will be holding my rifle."

Laughing Deer spoke again, and the headman responded.

"He said bring your rifle, but point it to the ground so it does not accidentally go off."

Laughing Deer stayed inside watching them as Victor came out and stood near his wife's window so she could interpret for him.

The headman spoke slowly and calmly. They come in peace, he said. They are the Tolkepaya people of the Yavapai tribe. They live in the highlands in the west. He knows the white man and his Navajo wife are peaceful people, because they have been watching them for three years. He is glad that the family has done well. Up in the mountains life is hard. Game is hard to come by. The herds of deer that used to run freely in the woods are now fewer, because miners also hunt them for food. The crops do not thrive. The corn, squash and beans do not yield enough to feed more than two families. They have been fighting Pima tribesmen who raid their villages and steal their food. The blue coat soldiers chase his people, calling them Apache, and killing their young braves. His people are hungry. Children cry to their mothers for food but there is no food to give. They do not want to steal. He is asking for help.

"Tell him I understand what he said. I will go in now and talk to my wife."

Laughing Deer told him, and Victor went back inside the house. He was there for a long time, and the Indians were getting restless and apprehensive. They were constantly watching the horizon for any signs of blue coat soldiers. When Victor came out again, he did not bring his rifle. The headman noted this as a good sign.

"Tell him I will give him ten sheep and ten sacks of corn for each of them to carry."

After Laughing Deer told the headman, there was a sound of relief from the warriors. Victor thought he saw a tear in the corner of the headman's eye.

The tribesmen never came back again to bother them. It must have taken a lot out of them just to ask for help.

CHAPTER IV

News that the war between the Northern and Southern states had ended reached the valley weeks after General Robert E. Lee surrendered to General Ulysses Grant at the Appomattox. Several months after that, not much had changed at the McCall farm, but the population in the town had grown with displaced Southern families and drifters. Shooting incidents and robbery were almost a daily occurrence. But the mining companies had thrived, increasing their productivity by hauling goods with wagon teams, back and forth between the mines and the ships plying the Colorado River. The rumor was that companies were shipping gold to other states for processing where it would be safer.

Jeremiah was playing in the field when from a great distance he saw a swirl of dust rise up the air.

"Mother, there's a dust storm coming."

"Where?"

"It's coming from the west."

Laughing Deer came to look. There was a cloud of dust from a distance, but it was not a storm. It was a group of men on horseback chasing a wagon.

"Call your father."

"I'm here, I saw it," Victor said, having come from the field. "Get inside."

Laughing Deer went inside, then came out again and handed

Victor his rifle. The wagon was coming in fast. A few more feet, and it would be within rifle range. Victor could now see the driver. It was a lanky young man with dark hair. The men chasing him looked Mexican. They were shooting at the man on the wagon. There were more gangs of bandits roaming around since the end of the war. Some of them were drifters from the south, some Mexicans, and some northerners looking to rob miners of their gold rather than pan for it themselves.

Victor took aim and brought down two bandits in succession. There was a sound of a rifle shot from behind him, and he turned to see Laughing Deer shooting from the window. He turned again in time to see a Mexican fall off his horse.

The wagon came to a quick halt in front of their house. The young man jumped off and immediately dropped two men from their horses with two successive shots.

The bandits turned and rode away.

"Thanks for your help, sir, ma'am."

"Looks like you didn't need our help. You're quite handy with those six-shooters."

"Lucky shots, that's all."

"What's your name, son?"

"Earp, sir. Wyatt Berry Stapp Earp."

"That's quite a long name."

"Yes, sir. My father named me after Captain Wyatt Berry Stapp, his commanding officer in the Illinois Mounted Volunteer during the Mexican-American War. Please just call me Wyatt."

"Pleased to make your acquaintance, Wyatt. My name is McCall. Victor McCall. That there is my wife, Laughing Deer."

"Pleased to meet you, sir," shaking his hand, "Ma'am."

Jeremiah came out the door. He wanted to be introduced too.

"And, who is this handsome young man?"

"That's Jeremiah, our son. Say hello to Mr. Earp, Jeremiah."

"Call me Wyatt, Jeremiah,"

"I have an Indian name."

"Really? What is it?"

"Little Wolf."

"That is a very nice name, Little Wolf. What will I call you then?"

"Either one."

"Then I will call you Either One."

Jeremiah giggled, then said," You're funny, Mr. Earp."

"Wyatt."

"Wyatt."

Turning to Victor McCall, he said, "Thank you again Mr. McCall. It's best for me to get under way while it's still light."

"Where are you bound for?"

"I'm delivering some cargo to Prescott."

"It will be dark before you get there. Why don't you stay the night, food will be ready soon. Those Mexican bandits might still be out there waiting for you. The U.S. soldiers from Fort Whipple will be out on patrol in the morning. That would be a better time for you to go."

"I don't want to impose, sir."

"No imposition," Laughing Deer said. "You are more than welcome to stay and have supper with us."

"Thank you ma'am. Yes, I would like to stay, if Either One approves."

Jeremiah giggled. "You are funny Wyatt."

At supper, conversation drifted to the work Wyatt was doing.

"My older brother, Virgil, and I worked as stagecoach drivers for the Banning Stage Line in California. It was a good job and paid enough for our upkeep. There are eleven of us in the family, including my father Nicholas and my mother Virginia. We all work where there is work to find. We have lived in Kentucky, Illinois, Iowa and California."

"How old are you, son?" Victor asked casually.

"Nineteen, sir."

"How did you end up doing what you're doing now?"

"I heard that they were looking for teamster drivers to move cargo from the Colorado River boats and deliver them to their final destinations overland. The company offered much higher pay."

"Do you like what you're doing?"

"There are bandits all over who are always looking to take your cargo away from you. I don't mind the risk. I can handle that. But, I miss my family. We were always together, except during the war when my older brothers went away to join the Union soldiers. I tried to enlist too, but they didn't want me on account that I was only thirteen years old."

"What happened to your brother?"

"James returned home in '63 after being wounded badly in Fredericktown, Missouri. Newton and Virgil did not return home until the war ended."

"Have you seen them yet?"

"Briefly. Right before I left."

"You seem to have a nice family, Wyatt. I hope everything works out well for all of you."

"I hope so too, sir."

"Well, it's getting late. You will want to have an early start. Why don't we call it a night, and turn in. Jeremiah, say goodnight to Wyatt and go to bed. Your mother will be in shortly to tuck you in."

"Goodnight, Wyatt."

"Goodnight, Either One."

"You're funny."

The young man, Wyatt Earp, became a regular visitor to the McCall farm in the next two years. For some reason, he saw in them what he was missing—a family. Whenever he was hauling cargo to their area he would stop by, always bringing little gifts for the family, and news about what was going on in the big towns. Most of the time, he would have supper with them and stay overnight, unless he came early in the day and had a long distance to travel to make a delivery.

"The towns are getting bigger, and all sorts of men and women come in everyday. Some of them come on the riverboats. Cattlemen, gamblers, miners—all sorts of drifters. There are a lot of rough people out there, Mr. McCall. They fight and steal from each other. They're gunslingers who would shoot people with the slightest provocation. I would suggest for you and your family to avoid the towns, unless it's really necessary to go."

Winter was setting in, and Victor McCall had already stocked up with the necessary provisions to see them through until spring. He agreed with Wyatt Earp to avoid the towns for a while. There was no need for a visit anyhow.

Later, the conversation centered on the Earp family, as it always did.

"How are they doing?" Victor asked, seriously concerned for their welfare.

"My people moved again from California to join my uncle, Jonathan Douglas, in Lamar, Missouri. My father found work as constable in that town. He wrote me a letter and wants me to join them."

"Are you going to?"

"I am considering it."

CHAPTER V

In the summer of 1868, the McCall household had a surprise visitor. He came down from the northeastern mountain with twelve heavily armed companions, crossed the river, and went directly to front of the house. The night was moonless and the sky was overcast. From behind the gun port, Victor could not make out who the visitors were. A week earlier, a raiding party of Zuni came swooping down from the east and stole the horses. But, this group did not rush in as the Zunis did. They simply rode in quietly, and sat on their horses in front of the house.

"It must be the Tolkepaya tribe needing more help," Victor said.

"No, these came from the northeastern mountain, not the west, and their horses look different. But, I think I know those horses."

"Laughing Deer, it is I, Wrestling Bear!" the leader shouted.

"It's my brother!"

Laughing Deer did not wait for Victor to say anything. She rushed to the door, flung it wide open, and tearfully ran toward her brother. Wrestling Bear jumped off his horse to greet his sister.

"Control yourself, woman!" Wrestling Bear chided. "There is no need for tears."

Victor came out with Jeremiah.

"Greetings my brother," Wrestling Bear said.

"Greetings. What brings you this far south?"

"I bring good news," Wrestling Bear said as he picked up Jeremiah.

"How is Little Wolf?"

"Little Wolf, that is your uncle Wrestling Bear. Now do you remember him?" Laughing Deer said to Jeremiah, calling him Little Wolf, which she always did in the presence of the tribe.

"Yes, I remember."

"How old are you now?" Wrestling Bear asked.

"Six."

"Come inside, all of you. I have some food," Laughing Deer said, running to the door, then back out again.

"Come!"

Wrestling Bear ordered two warriors to stay outside to guard.

"So tell me, what is the news from Bosque Redondo?" Laughing Deer asked as soon as she served the food.

"The Diné are free people again," Wrestling Bear began. "Red Lance and Weaving Woman are safe. They live outside Fort Defiance."

"What happened?" Victor asked.

"Our people were sick and dying at Bosque Redondo. Most of the Apache who were also living there escaped with their chief, Victorio. We learned that the Great White Father in Washington himself was not happy with the affairs at Fort Sumner. Then *Bihkehhe*, War Chief Stanton, recalled General James Carleton, and sent General William Tecumseh Sherman in his place."

"General James Carleton was the one who ordered Colonel Kit Carson to round up your people in '64, and move them to Fort Sumner in New Mexico. He was a hard man to deal with," Victor McCall said, remembering how the general refused to even see him when he was appealing for the release of Laughing Deer and her family.

"General Sherman. What kind of a man is he?" Laughing Deer asked.

"He listens. He saw how it was at Bosque Redondo. The water was bad, and food was not enough. Nothing grew well. The Comanche would come from Texas and raid the reservation. Our people had no guns to protect themselves and their property. The soldiers did not care. Those soldiers, they raped our women, and our women would get sick with disease they got from them. Then, our men would get sick too, for sleeping with their wives."

"God, that is ghastly!" Victor McCall said. "I had no idea it was that bad."

Laughing Deer looked at her husband, but did not say anything.

"The Navajo chiefs and headmen gathered together and decided that Chief Barboncito should speak on behalf of the tribe to General Sherman, and request that the tribe is sent back to our homeland. General Sherman listened, then said he would talk to the Great White Father in Washington."

"I'm happy the general was willing to listen to Chief Barboncito," Laughing Deer said.

"Chief Barboncito speaks well. No other chief speaks better than Chief Barboncito in tribal councils," Wrestling Bear said. "He chooses his words well, and speaks with great wisdom."

"What did Washington say?" Victor was now anxious to know.

"Many days after, General Sherman said he had sent army engineers to survey good lands in Oklahoma and Kansas. 'Your people will be happy in the new place,' the general said."

"So it was either Oklahoma or Kansas," Victor said.

"The chiefs were not happy. They wanted to go home to our own land. Chief Barboncito pleaded with General Sherman, using great words, and explained how the Navajo cannot live well in any other place but the land where the First Woman put our people. The land is not just a land, he said. It is holy. It is part of the whole being of the Navajo nation. At Diné Land the people are in harmony with Mother Earth and Father Sky, and all the creatures living there. If we are moved to another place we will die, just as we are dying in Bosque Redondo. That is what he said to General Sherman."

"What did General Sherman say? Was he angry?" Laughing Deer asked.

"They talked for many days and many nights. Then General

Sherman said that all the chiefs had to agree not to make any more war against the United States' government. Then they signed a treaty, General Sherman and all the Navajo chiefs and headmen. It took a long time before Chief Manuelito was persuaded by the other chiefs to sign the treaty. Without his signature there would be no treaty."

"So, the general agreed?" Victor McCall said.

Laughing Deer made a sighing sound as if she had been holding her breathe for a long time.

"We were given back our land, but only a small part of it," Wrestling Bear continued. "White settlers had already taken over the farms and land that were abandoned when our people were moved to Bosque Redondo."

They were all silent for a long time after Wrestling Bear finished.

"Finally, it's over," Victor McCall said after a while. Then he looked at his wife, and their eyes met.

"My husband, we must go and visit Red Lance and Weaving Woman," Laughing Deer finally said.

"Yes, we will as soon as we can make the necessary arrangements to keep the farm going."

Laughing Deer was beside herself with excitement. She had kept all her fears and concerns for her family and her people to herself all these years. Now she could see that things would be all right.

"You have a corral but no horses, my brother. Why is that?"

"The Zuni came one night and stole all of them."

"How many horses?"

"Twenty."

Wrestling Bear and his warriors stayed a long time after they had finished supper. He and his sister had much to talk about.

"You must come back and live in Diné Land. It is not good to live away from your home," Wrestling Bear said.

"We have made a home here, my brother."

"But this is not your home. You are still a stranger here"

"This is my husband's home. I live where he lives."

"You do not receive the blessings and the protection of the Holy

People if you live here."

"We have done well in four years. We receive the blessings and protection of my husband's Holy People."

"You have always been a stubborn woman!"

"I know you mean well, my brother. Please do not worry. We are well."

"We must go now before our enemies know we are here. I will come back again soon," Wrestling Bear finally said.

He stood up and said goodbye to Victor McCall and Little Wolf. They left as quietly as they came.

"I am going out for a while," Laughing Deer said after Wrestling Bear left.

Victor McCall did not say anything. He had learned to understand his wife's quiet moods. A little while later, they heard Laughing Deer singing in the hogan.

"What is she singing, father?"

"I believe it is called the Night Way."

"What is it for?"

"It's a ritual to restore *Hozhó*—balance and harmony in the Navajo world."

"Oh."

Jeremiah was satisfied with the answer his father gave him, although he did not fully understand what restoring balance in the Navajo world meant.

Laughing Deer stayed in the hogan all night, singing Night Way songs until sunrise.

Five nights later, Wrestling Bear was back with his warriors, driving a herd of horses directly into the McCall corral. He and his warriors had painted their faces with different colors and designs.

"Now, you have horses in your corral," Wrestling Bear said.

"These are Zuni horses!" Laughing Deer said, recognizing the paint designs.

"They are your horses."

"But there are twenty five of them," Victor McCall said.

"The five horses are gifts from the Zunis for causing you trouble. Guard all of them well, so they don't steal them again from you."

"Thank you," Victor said.

"I will tell Red Lance and Weaving Woman that you are all well."

"Goodbye, my brother," Laughing Deer said, choking on her words.

"Woman, control yourself!"

CHAPTER VI

Jeremiah watched every time his father drove in a herd of mustangs from the canyon. Victor McCall had been successful in capturing the mustangs, breaking them in, then selling them to the army at Fort Whipple, and to the stagecoach company. It was profitable, but hard work for one man. When Jeremiah was seven, his father started taking him along when he tracked and captured mustangs. He helped his father bring them in. Soon, he was breaking in mustangs himself. He had no fear whatever, and even with his small stature he stayed on and held well until the mustangs had calmed down.

There were days when Jeremiah went off on his own. He would ride out to the prairie and to the far mountains on a mustang that he broke in and trained, and lose himself among the tall pines. Other days he explored old, deserted mines that dotted the hills. One day, he came upon a mining camp that was almost hidden by the tall trees.

There were people working at that mine who looked different, and dressed different. They also talked to each other in words that he did not understand. When he first saw them at the mine an older man stopped working, smiled and spoke to him.

"*Ni hao ma*," the old man said.

Jeremiah sat there on his horse and smiled, but said nothing.

"Little boy, I just said how are you?" the old man said in halting English.

"I'm sorry sir, I did not understand."

"I said it in Chinese. Played a little trick on you."

"What is Chinese, sir?"

"That is my language. I'm Chinese, from country called China."

"Where is China?"

"Far away, across ocean."

"Ocean?"

"Big river. Big, big river."

"Oh, yes. Now I remember. My father is from Ireland. He said it is on the other side of the ocean. Is China near Ireland?"

"Across ocean, but not near Ireland. Other side. Farther away."

"Are they all from China?"

"Yes, all Chinese. Bossman American."

"*Ni hao ma,*" Jeremiah said slowly.

"*Wo hen hao*—fine, thank you. Little boy you learn fast."

"*Wo hen hao,*" Jeremiah said.

The old man laughed, amused.

"What is your name?"

"Jeremiah, sir. I am also called Little Wolf by my mother."

"*Pequeño Lobo.*"

"What was that, sir?"

"*Pequeño Lobo.* That is what the Mexicans will call you."

"You speak Mexican?"

"Spanish. *Sí*, I speak little Spanish. I learn where I work."

"What is your name, sir?"

"Abe Lincoln."

"Abe Lincoln?"

The old man smiled.

"I played a little trick on you again. My name is Lee Bok."

"Lee Bok."

"Yes, no trick. I have to go back to work now. You are nice boy. Come again. Visit."

"Yes, sir. I would love to."

Visiting the mining camp became a regular routine for Jeremiah.

Late one afternoon, after completing his chores for the day, Jeremiah went to visit the mine. There was a lot of commotion going on. Two men with no shirts were kicking and punching each other.

"What is happening, sir? Why are they fighting?"

"Not fighting. Practicing *Kung-Fu Wushu*. When bossman leaves, I teach young men *Kung-Fu Wushu*." Lee Bok said.

"What is *Kung-Fu Wushu*?"

"Chinese boxing. Good for fighting. Secret. Teach only to Chinese. Not tell bossman."

After that, Jeremiah would come later in the day when the Chinese men were practicing *Kung-Fu Wushu*.

"Can you teach me?" Jeremiah asked Lee Bok.

"No, Jeremiah. Teach only Chinese. Secret."

Jeremiah was disappointed. He wanted to learn *Kung-Fu Wushu*, as they called it. He had seen men fight with their fists in town, but this looked different. He watched the Chinese men everyday, and then practiced the moves they were doing when he got home. One day, he forgot where he was and started doing the moves the young men were doing as they were doing it. He heard laughter and clapping. The young men had stopped practicing and were watching him. Jeremiah stopped, embarrassed for being caught.

"*Shifu*, Jeremiah is very good," one young man said. "How long have you been teaching him *Kung-Fu*?"

"I not teach him!" Lee Bok seemed angry. "Who was teaching you?"

"Nobody. I'm sorry Lee Bok. I wanted to learn so I watched what they do."

Everybody was silent.

"If you want to learn, learn properly. Go, join the class."

"I can join the class?"

"Go!"

"Thanks, Lee Bok."

"From now on call me *Shifu*!"

"Shifu?"

"Master. All my students call me *Shifu*—Master. Give respect to teacher."

One day, the class was doing a breathing exercise. Jeremiah simply followed as best as he could what the other students were doing.

"What is the exercise called, *Shifu*?" Jeremiah asked.

"Exercise called *Chi Kung*."

"*Chi Kung*?"

"Yes, strengthen *Chi* inside body."

"What is *Chi*?"

"Energy inside body."

"*Chi* is energy inside my body," Jeremiah said.

"Yes. There is *Chi* inside body. There is *Chi* in plants you eat. There is *Chi* in air you breathe. *Chi* is all around you. Energy."

"And *Chi Kung* strengthens *Chi* inside my body."

"*Chi Kung* balances *Yin Yang* in *Chi*."

"*Yin Yang*?"

"*Chi*, energy, has *Yin* and *Yang*. Two parts. Soft and hard. When *Yin* is stronger than *Yang*, no good. When *Yang* is stronger than *Yin*, no good. *Chi* must be balanced between *Yin* and *Yang* or you get sick. *Chi Kung* balances *Yin* and *Yang* in *Chi*."

Jeremiah remembered his mother singing the Night Way songs in the hogan after the visit of Wrestling Bear the year before. His father had explained that the songs were to restore balance in the Navajo world. Jeremiah thought that it really was to balance *Yin Yang*, so the Navajo world would not get sick. Now he thought he understood.

That day it was near sundown by the time he reached home. The idea of *Chi* and *Yin Yang* had preoccupied him all the way as he rode down the mountain. He was looking forward to telling his mother what *Shifu* had told him. Then he realized that he had never even mentioned to his parents that he was learning *Kung-Fu Wushu*. Secret, he remembered Lee Bok saying. Teach only Chinese people.

"I stopped by to say goodbye."

Jeremiah heard a familiar voice as he walked in.

"Wyatt!"

"Hello, Either One."

"You are joining your family!" Laughing Deer said.

"Yes. Lamar, Missouri it is."

"We will miss you," Victor said.

"You have all been very kind to me. I can never thank you enough."

"You will stay and have supper with us," Laughing Deer said.

"Thank you kindly ma'am, but I would like to be on my way before sundown, for personal reasons. I will write when I am settled down in Missouri."

He paused for a while, and then said, "I almost forgot. There is a favor I would like to ask Either One. Pardon me."

Wyatt went out and took a sack from the back of his saddle and carefully opened it.

"I have a long way to travel, and I hope to find a good home for my little friend here."

"Mother, Lhachaeh!" Jeremiah cried out.

"Lhachaeh?" Wyatt looked at Laughing Deer inquiringly.

"He means dog,"

"Will Either One give Lhachaeh a home?"

"Yes, yes! Mother, Lhachaeh!"

"He has always wanted a dog," Victor said. "I just could not find one in town. Thank you. You made him very happy."

"It's a German Shepherd. Less than two months old."

"Thank you, Wyatt."

"You're welcome Either One. I best be going Mr. McCall, ma'am."

"Wait. If you cannot stay to have supper with us then you can take your supper with you. It will take only a minute."

Laughing Deer quickly wrapped some food and handed it to Wyatt.

"There."

"Thank you again for your kindness. Please take care of yourselves."

"You too, Wyatt."

CHAPTER VII

Jeremiah McCall could see the giant shadow of his father cast against the wall by the bright orange light of the flame from the burning barn on the opposite side of the house. The crackling sounds of Winchester rifles tore through the air. There were also the quick succession of explosions from six-shooters coming from outside. The team horses were neighing and stomping in the barn, possibly trying to break loose from their tethers. Lhachaeh kept barking at the window. Jeremiah was sure his German shepherd yearling could smell the men, and probably sensed that they were running closer to the house. His mother momentarily stopped firing her Winchester, and looked in his direction where he was crouched by the back door. Then she ran over, stooping low to dodge the bullets. She grabbed the blanket on the rocking chair, and threw it over Jeremiah.

"Whatever happens, be very quiet, son. Do you understand?"

Jeremiah nodded just before his mother covered him completely with the blanket. With his tiny frame, he looked like a piece of rag thrown into a corner. A small hole in the blanket, hardly large enough for his eye, afforded him a view of what was going on without exposing himself.

"I'm out of bullets," He heard his mother say.

Suddenly the door burst open, and two men with black hoods rushed in, followed by more hooded men shooting wildly all over the room. Victor McCall cut down the first two men as they barged in. Two other men aimed their six-shooters and fired four or five shots each, throwing Victor McCall back against the wall, killing him instantly.

"Damn fool of a squaw man," one of the men said.

Laughing Deer screamed as she saw her husband going down. She grabbed the butt of her empty rifle, and swung at the nearest man bringing him down to his knee. Another man grabbed the gun away from her and slapped her hard, knocking her unconscious.

Lhachaeh immediately attacked the man who slapped Laughing Deer, sinking its teeth hard into the soft flesh of his arm. The big dog was growling loud, its eyes wild with anger.

"Sonofabitch! Shoot the dog! Shoot the dog," the bitten man kept yelling.

There was a loud bang of a six-shooter, and the dog flew across the room toward the back door. It landed on the floor with a thud, crawled a few more feet then collapsed with its paw covering the blanket under which Jeremiah was hidden.

"Shoot it again, Tom!"

"What fer? It's dead."

"Just shoot it!"

"You shoot it! I want this woman!"

"Hell, no. I go first." The man was heavy-set and had a croaky voice. He took off his hood because he was sweating profusely. "I'll enjoy this better with this goddamn thing off my face."

The other man was already on top of Laughing Deer tearing off her clothes.

"Get off her."

The other man ignored what he said.

"Tom, I said I go first."

The man called Tom kept tearing off Laughing Deer's clothes.

"I swear to God, I'll shoot your prick off!"

Then he gave the man called Tom a strong kick in the side of the ribs with the sole of his boots.

"Aw, goddamn, Jesse. That really hurts."

"Next time, you listen."

Jesse straddled Laughing Deer.

"She's damn good looking for a squaw."

"What difference does it make? She is a squaw. Get on with it, I want my turn too."

"Nice long hair. Would look good on my belt. I want that scalp later."

When the last man was finished with Laughing Deer, the man asked, "What d'ya want to do with her, Jesse, take her with us?"

"Ya want to be a squaw man, too? Dumb. I'll take care of the woman," he said taking out his knife. "Take off your hoods and search the house for his stash of gold. McCall has a pile somewhere. He never gambled or spent much in town."

"I never saw him go to the bank either," the man called Tom said with a chuckle. "He's got his money here somewhere, alright."

"Look under the bed, tear up the wall planks." Jesse kept barking orders.

The men kept walking back and forth, throwing things on the floor, turning boxes and furniture over. At one point a man stood almost on top of where Jeremiah was covered with the blanket.

Jeremiah could now see their faces. He recognized some them from their visits in town. A couple of them also had been at the corral twice, bargaining to buy some mustangs for the mines.

"Got it!" one man shouted, holding up a small sack he found in a box. "There's more in here. Damn, this man rich!"

"Good. Now burn the house down, and let's go. Let the soldiers think the damn Injuns did it," the man called Jesse ordered as he walked out the door.

One man started breaking the oil lamps and spilling oil all over the floor. Another man threw a lighted match on the oil, which immediately burst into flame. Then they ran outside.

"Get the horses, and let's get out of here," Jesse said.

"Wait a minute. Didn't they have a little boy?" one of the men said.

"He is probably dead from all that shooting," another man said.

"I didn't see a body, did you?" Jesse said.

"If he ain't dead from the shooting, he is probably dead now in that fire," Tom said.

"What's in the that Injun hut?" Jesse asked, pointing to the hogan.

"Nothing worth anything," somebody said.

"Burn it too."

Jeremiah heard horses galloping away. The flames were now high near the front door. He stood up and made a move toward his mother, but the heat stopped him. He retreated toward the back door, tiptoed to reach for the latch and pushed the door open. Cool air bellowed in, making the fire burn higher. With all the strength he could muster, Jeremiah dragged Lhachaeh, slowly, inch by inch, until they were safely out of the house, and at some distance from the fire. Then he collapsed on the ground and fell asleep beside Lhachaeh.

When he awoke, the sun was already up. He felt someone lifting him, and he cautiously opened his eyes.

"You are awake."

It was Wrestling Bear.

"We saw fire in the night. What happened?"

"Mother. Where's mother?

"Mother dead. Father, too."

"Lhachaeh. Where is Lhachaeh?"

"Dog hurt but alive. What happened?"

"Men came last night wearing black hoods," Jeremiah held back his tears, remembering Wrestling Bear once said to him that tears were for women.

"They called out to father. I could not understand what they were saying," he continued. "Somebody kept yelling "squaw man." Father would not come out, and they started shooting at the house. Then they burned the barn while the horses were in there. I saw them shooting the sheep, killing them one by one. They were laughing. Father blew out the lamps and gave a rifle to mother. They started shooting back at the men. I saw two men shot off their horses. Father shouted to stay away from the window. I ran to the back of the room near the back door and mother came over and covered me with a blanket. She told me to be very quiet. Somebody broke down the door and two men entered the house. I saw father kill them. Then two other men came in and shot father. They kept shooting and shooting. A lot more men came in. A big man, called Jesse, slapped mother, and a thin man shot Lhachaeh. The thin man was called Tom. Then they hurt mother. They took off their hoods, and I saw their faces. I had seen them before. The man called Jesse told them to look for father's gold. They started throwing things around the house. Somebody yelled he found the gold and then they burned the house and rode away."

"I saw tracks. There were many men. Your father fought bravely. He was a true warrior."

Wrestling Bear paused for a while.

"Your mother was a good wife to your father. Stayed with him to the end," he finally said.

Jeremiah looked at his uncle and the ten men with him. Their faces were not painted. It was not a war party. It was a hunting party.

"We must go. There is nothing more in here for you."

CHAPTER VIII

When they reached the top of the hill, Jeremiah looked back to the valley below. His eyes followed the river as it swerved farther away and rested on the charred remains of their house and the hogan. He blinked several times to brush away the image of the fire in his mind—his father being thrown back against the wall by the force of the close range explosion of the guns, Lhachaeh flying in the air as if blown back by the wind, and his mother lying on the floor with men on top of her, hurting her. He could see the dead sheep scattered all around in the field. The team horses were in their stalls in the barn. He could see parts of the stalls, all charred, but he could not make out the horses. The mustangs in the outer corral were all gone.

Wrestling Bear turned to look at Jeremiah, who was riding with a warrior on his pony, and followed the direction he was looking, but he did not say anything. He turned and kept riding on silently, as did the other warriors.

They traveled for ten days, stopping only for water, a brief rest, and a light meal of dried venison. The nights were chilly, but it was too dangerous to build a fire with enemies all around. The warriors hunted along the way, never separating from the main party for more than two hours. Food had been scarce in Navajo land since Colonel Kit Carson and his soldiers burned the fields and killed the livestock four years before. Hundreds of warriors were killed in the fight. Thousands of the survivors, mostly old men, women and children, were rounded up and forced to march four hundred miles from Arizona to Bosque Redondo at Fort Sumner, New Mexico. The land was slowly recovering now, but the yield was still not sufficient to feed the villages. Buffalo herds had been fast disappearing with white hunters killing them for their hides. The Navajo warriors had to travel for miles and days just to hunt small game. They even hunted outside their traditional land.

"Tell more what you remember," Wrestling Bear said to Little Wolf as they rode. "Tell me about the men."

Little Wolf described the men. For a boy his age, he showed an unusual attention to details. He described their faces, what they wore, and their build. They went over and over the descriptions until Wrestling Bear felt he had a complete picture of everyone. The only thing missing was the names of all of them.

As they reached the gullies, the hunters returned to the main party. They had seen a band of Ute camped at the north end of the arroyo.

"It's a raiding party," they reported to Wrestling Bear. "They have sheep and horses, and Navajo women and children captives."

"How many captives?"

"Three women and two children."

"How many braves?"

"Fifteen."

"Any soldiers in the area?"

"We have not seen the blue coats since we left camp."

"Sheep will slow us down, but our people need them."

Wrestling Bear looked at Jeremiah. He was concerned about the danger to the boy, but he had his responsibility to his people as a leader of a band of warriors.

"We will attack," Wrestling Bear finally said.

The warriors were happy with the decision, but restrained themselves from letting out a war cry. The sound carried in the canyons, and they knew the importance of silence if they were to surprise the enemy.

Wrestling Bear walked over to Jeremiah.

"All the braves are coming. I cannot leave you here by yourself. It is safer for you to come along. Later, you will watch the horses. You must stay quiet."

Jeremiah nodded.

The band started walking silently into the canyon, holding the reins of their horses behind them. At the bend an hour later, Wrestling Bear said, "This a good place to leave the horses. Run a rope across the path and tie the horses to the rope. The rope will stop the Ute horses from escaping this way."

Wrestling Bear took the dog from the warrior who was carrying it, and laid it beside Little Wolf. Turning to the boy he said, "Listen to the sounds around you. Do not sleep, or the enemy will be upon you."

Little Wolf was tired, but the words reminded him of what his mother used to say, "Do not sleep, or the enemy will be upon you."

"Here. Take the tomahawk"

The band moved on before Little Wolf could say anything. Now he must remain completely silent. The wait was long, and Little Wolf was having a hard time keeping his eyes open. He rested his head on the ground. He looked at the sky. He could make out the jagged edges of the canyon top silhouetted against the moonlit clouds. He loved the mountains. At his father's farm he would play out in the fields with Lhachaeh, and look far out to the distant snow-capped mountain tops, imagining himself reaching out and touching them. The thought kept him preoccupied for a while. But now, in the dark, he began to feel the pangs of loneliness. He was cold. He missed his mother. He remembered how Laughing Deer would wrap a blanket around him and hold him close to her on a cold night like this. He remembered his father fighting the hooded men. His father was very brave, he thought. He remembered the bright flames, the man shooting his dog, and the big man holding his mother's scalp. He began to feel a kind of anger that he had never felt before. It was different from the times he got angry with Lhachaeh when he would not sit and stay. Tears started flowing from his eyes. Tears are only for women, he kept reminding himself. Then he began to sob.

He must have fallen asleep. He was in an arroyo huddled together with his mother and many women and children. He climbed up the low embankment when his mother looked away for a second. He could see flames go higher and higher in the cornfields all around. There was a lot of shouting and screaming. Babies were crying. Men in blue coats were wrestling with Navajo men. Guns exploding. Arrows were flying around. There were big guns being pulled by horses. These made the loudest noise—like thunder. When they exploded, the ground shook. A big fire and smoke came out of their noses, and Navajo men would fly and fall down.

His mother pulled him down from the embankment.

"You must keep your head down, and stay quiet."

All of a sudden, the shooting stopped. There were the sounds of horses galloping back and forth and men talking in his father's language.

"Where is father? How come he is not here?" Jeremiah whispered.

"He is away on business. He will come for us. Do not talk anymore."

"Colonel Carson, there are warriors still holding out in the canyon," a soldier was talking to a mustachioed man with a buckskin coat who sat tall on a big horse just above the embankment. "Tell them to surrender now or we will burn them out."

"Yes sir!"

"Search every nook and cranny men. Look down the crevices. Enter all the caves. General Carleton ordered that nobody be left behind except the dead."

"Sir, there are women and children down here in the arroyo."

"Bring them out and line them up."

"Do not fall asleep, or the enemy will be upon you," Jeremiah heard his mother's voice.

"I wasn't asleep. I just closed my eyes."

He raised his head. There was nobody there. He was sure he had not been asleep, but his mother was not there. He was all alone. The clouds covered the moon, and it was dark.

The horses were getting restless, digging their hooves on the ground. War cries and loud screaming echoed from the far end of the canyon. Then there was a thundering sound of hooves approaching—it got louder and louder. Little Wolf stood up to look. A herd of horses was coming his way fast. There was one warrior on a horse leading the pack. It was an Ute brave.

The herd stopped all of sudden at the tether and started milling around, confused. The Navajo horses blocked their way. The Ute jumped off his horse and drew his knife. He was about to cut the rope when he noticed Little Wolf standing there. He ran toward the boy, the knife still in his hand. Little Wolf braced himself and threw the tomahawk at the warrior. The Ute stopped and looked surprised. The tomahawk was lodged in his forehead. He fell face down.

A few seconds later, Wrestling Bear came galloping in on an Ute horse.

"Little Wolf. Where are you?"

He quickly dismounted when he saw Little Wolf. For a second, he thought the Ute crouched on the ground was going to attack. Then he realized the warrior was dead, a tomahawk almost splitting his head. He looked at Little Wolf, drew his knife and slit off the enemy's scalp. Then he held it out for Little Wolf to take.

"This is your kill. You earned the scalp."

Little Wolf stood there not knowing what he was supposed to do.

"Take it!"

He took the scalp slowly. He was confused.

"The warrior blood runs strong in your veins," Wrestling Bear said proudly. "You are now a man. From now on, you will be called by your warrior name, Little Man Wolf."

He let out a loud victory war cry that echoed through the canyon. From the far end, the victory cries of the Navajo warriors echoed back to them."

CHAPTER IX

The Ute warriors they just killed had taken those captives, sheep, and horses from the Navajo clans in Canyon de Chelly. The women wanted to go back home on their own, but Wrestling Bear wisely told them they would only be prey again to enemy bands.

"We are going to Fort Defiance. We will make arrangements from there to bring you back to Canyon de Chelly."

After nine days, they reached the Navajo village, just outside Fort Defiance. It was a cluster of fifteen hogans. In the past, the Navajo tended to live apart from each other. Spanish missionaries taught them to plant corn and raise sheep. The flocks also needed large pastures, but that was all gone. As families slowly returned to their homeland from the Bosque Redondo reservation, they converged near Fort Defiance for their food ration and protection from their enemies. The United States soldiers promised to protect the Navajo in the treaty with General William Tecumseh Sherman. But out on the prairie, the soldiers did not distinguish among roving bands of Indians and could just as easily turn against them.

Wrestling Bear took Jeremiah directly to Padre Tomas, the old priest at the mission. Padre Tomas was an Irish Priest whose name was Father Thomas. After Mexico ceded its claim to New Mexico, the American missionaries took over the conversion of the natives. It was still easier for a Navajo to use the Spanish names.

"Padre Tomas, this is my nephew Little Man Wolf."

Wrestling Bear was now calling him by his warrior name.

"He has just lost his mother, my sister Laughing Deer, and his father Victor McCall. White men in black hoods killed them and destroyed their home. Little Man Wolf will live with my mother, Weaving Woman, and my father, Red Lance. He will learn the ways of the Navajo, but I would also like him to learn the ways of his white father. It would be a great honor if he can learn from you. He is only eight years old, Padre, but he is already a man. An Ute scalp hangs on his belt. We think he will not grow much taller than he is now, but he is strong, quick and wise for his age. Soon he will be even stronger. He will be able to help you. He already speaks his father's language and his mother's tongue. His parents taught him well."

Padre Tomas glanced at the scalp on Little Man Wolf's belt.

"Of course, my son. Your nephew is welcome here. Do you have a Christian name, Little Man Wolf?"

"My father called me Jeremiah McCall, sir," he said shyly.

"Yes, of course, Jeremiah. I'm happy to finally meet you. I knew your father, and I watched your mother grow up to be a beautiful and fine woman. I am sorry for your loss. God loves all his children, my son. He looks after all of us. He has a purpose and a plan for each one of us. Remember that. He has brought you here. You are safe here with me and your people."

"Thank you Padre," Wrestling Bear said. "I cannot stay long. The soldiers have been looking for Chief Manuelito and any band roaming around. I do not want to bring trouble to my people here."

"Where will you go now?"

"First I must take Little Man Wolf to Weaving Woman and Red Lance and tell them what happened. When he is ready, Red Lance will bring Little Man Wolf back to you. He will do whatever it is you ask him to do. My band will return to Chief Manuelito's camp after they distribute the food they brought for their families. I will go back to McCall's farm to finish something. It is best I travel alone. It attracts less attention."

"The Mexicans, the Pueblo and the Ute are raiding Navajo camps, stealing sheep, cattle and horses, and taking captives for slaves. The new law against slavery has not stopped them. Be careful."

"Yes, I know Padre. We just saved three women and two children from the Ute. They were taken from Canyon de Chelly. But, for now, we will have to distribute them among families who can take care of them until they are strong enough for us to take them back to their own clans."

"Go then and do what you must do. *Vaya con Dios*."

CHAPTER X

Jeremiah McCall sat quietly in the hogan as Wrestling Bear, Weaving Woman and Red Lance spoke in low voices. The heat from the burning cedar log that was set in the middle of the floor was soothing and made him feel sleepy. He struggled to keep his eyes open. Although he understood the Navajo words, he was too tired to follow what was being said. He heard Wrestling Bear saying 'Victor McCall and Laughing Deer dead', 'house burned', 'sheep killed', 'horses gone.'

He also heard him say, "Little Wolf has made his first kill. An Ute scalp hangs in his belt. We now call him Little Man Wolf. He is a warrior."

"That is good," Red Lance said.

Weaving Woman asked about the captives waiting outside the hogan.

"They are from the clans living in Canyon de Chelly. I will leave them with you. They need to rest and regain their strength. The other captives have been distributed to other families."

"It is cold out. Bring them in, and let them rest by the fire," Weaving Woman said.

Wrestling Bear went out and brought in the woman and the girl.

"I am called Smiling Feathers and was born to Graceful Dove of the Water's Edge Clan and born for Prancing Horse of the Badlands People," the woman said. "This is my sister, Little Sunflower."

"How old are you?"

"I am sixteen years old. My sister is six."

"You are from Canyon de Chelly?"

"Yes, we live there with my mother's clan. Mother dead during march to Bosque Redondo."

"You are not married?"

"No."

"You are a beautiful woman."

Smiling Feathers glanced at Wrestling Bear, and then she quickly lowered her eyes.

"No unmarried men in our village. Most young warriors killed in the fight with soldiers at Canyon De Chelly. "

"Your father, where is he?"

"Prancing Horse also dead in the fight."

"You are welcome here. You may rest until you are strong again. Then if you wish to return to your clan, arrangements can be made. But, if you wish to stay with us, this is your home. You will be one of us." Weaving Woman said.

"I thank you, and I thank your son, Wrestling Bear, and his brave warriors for saving us."

"Now, you must eat so you will wake up feeling stronger."

"I brought venison meat, sheep and horses," Wrestling Bear said. "You may use them for yourselves, as you please, and as gift to the medicine man for any ceremony."

When Jeremiah woke up the next morning, Wrestling Bear was gone. He ran outside to look for him. Then he went back inside the hogan and stood waiting for Weaving Woman to notice him.

"Wrestling Bear did not stay last night, Little Man Wolf. He went back to your father's farm. He will be away for a long while. Now, be quiet and let the woman and child rest. I will take your food outside."

The next few days and nights were a blur. There was a lot of singing, dancing and drum beating. His grandparents were singing the loudest, and in high-pitched voices. The medicine man was there with his rattle and mask. He kept blowing smoke in Little Man Wolf's face. Finally, everything settled down.

Little Man Wolf, the woman and the child were not asked to do anything to help for several days.

During the day Red Lance would be up early tending the sheep, cattle, and horses. Then he would be off in the afternoon spear fishing in the lake, or hunting for small game. Weaving Woman checked the cornfield and tended the vegetable garden. In the afternoon, she weaved blankets. When the sun went down, she prepared their evening meal.

Smiling Feathers and Little Sunflower started helping with the vegetable garden, checking the cornfield, and preparing meals. When Weaving Woman rested from weaving, Smiling Feathers took over. She had already learned weaving from her mother. Little Man Wolf helped Red Lance tend the sheep, cattle, and horses. Lhachaeh, who was now fully recovered, was always watchful for strays and wolves that preyed on the sheep.

"A long, long time ago, as many nights as there are little lights in the sky, the Holy People created the Navajo People. They called us *Ni'hookaa Diyan Diné*, the Holy Earth People or Lords of the Earth." Weaving Woman spoke as she and Smiling Feathers tended to their cooking.

Little Man Wolf looked up from the floor when he realized his grandmother was talking to him. Lhachaeh also looked up. Little Sunflower came over and sat beside Little Man Wolf to listen.

"Outsiders call us Navajo, which is fine. But among ourselves, we simply say Diné—The People."

"Why do they call us Navajo?"

"The Tewa Indians used Navahu, which means The Large Area of Cultivated Land. The Zuni Indians call us Apache Du Navahu. Apache in Zuni is Enemy."

"Are the Zuni our enemy?"

"There are tribes that make war on us. They steal our sheep, cattle and horses and take captives to sell as slaves."

"The Zuni stole my father's horses once. Wrestling Bear and his warriors took them back," Little Man Wolf said.

"You have an Ute scalp hanging in your belt. So, you know Ute are also enemies," Weaving Woman said.

"The Ute captured me and Smiling Feathers. I could not run fast enough," Little Sunflower said.

Smiling Feathers remembered how brave and strong Wrestling Bear was. She saw him kill four Ute at the canyon, maybe more. She felt sorry that he had to leave so soon, and would be away for a long time.

"What about the Apache?" Little Man Wolf asked.

"The Apache are our cousins. Sometimes we fight as cousins do, but they are our relatives. We speak similar language. Now, go look for your grandfather and tell him food is ready."

The stories about the Navajo people continued every day and night. Weaving Woman told Little Man Wolf and Little Sunflower to sit and listen to her stories as she and Smiling Feathers wove blankets or prepared their meals.

"The Diné passed through three worlds before emerging into this present world," she began. "This was at the beginning of time—long, long ago. The First World was black. Masked spirits, insects and animals lived there. The First Man and First Woman were created there. The beings were constantly quarreling with each other, so the First Man and First Woman left through an opening in the east. Some insects and animals went with them as they entered into the Second World. This world was blue. The Blue Birds lived there, and made them feel unwanted. Life was hard in the blue world, and no one was happy. The First Man then made a magic wand of turquoise, white shell, jet, and abalone. He pointed it south, and it opened into the Third World. This world was yellow. The First Man and First Woman entered. The Coyote and other beings followed. The land had rivers running east, west, north and south. This was good land, but the Coyote who came with them had always been a troublemaker. One day, the Coyote stole the Water Baby from the river. The Water

Mother was very angry. She made the water rise higher and higher. The First Man told everyone to climb on the reed to rise up with the water. Then, they learned it was the Coyote that had stolen the Water Baby. All the beings were angry at the Coyote, and they ordered him to return the baby to the mother. He did and the water receded. As they climbed out of the reed, they stood at the entrance to the Fourth World. This was the present world, and it was glittering and white. The Locust was the first to enter, but there were already other beings there. They refused to let the First Man and First Woman and the other beings from the Third World enter unless the Locust agreed to some tests. The Locust passed all the tests, and all the beings from the Third World were allowed to enter the Glitter World. Then, the First Man and First Woman brought out the soil they carried from the First World, and with this they created the four sacred mountains that set the boundaries of Diné Land."

"Why are they sacred?" Little Sunflower asked.

"The Holy People, the First Man and the First Woman, created them and placed our people within these boundaries to be our home forever. Those mountains and this land they have given us are sacred to our people."

"Where are these mountains?" Little Man Wolf asked.

"In Colorado there is the Hesperus Peak in the north, and Blanca Peak in the east. In the south there is Mount Taylor in New Mexico. In the west, the San Francisco Peak in Arizona."

"So this is our land."

"Yes. The First Man and First Woman told the people never to leave this sacred homeland. If they leave, bad things will happen to them. If forced to leave, they will die. Here, our people will be in balance with Mother Earth, Sky Father, and the spiritual beings. Here we will prosper, and our people will be healthy."

"If we leave, will we die?" Little Man Wolf asked.

"Bad things will happen to you."

"But, our farm was not in Diné Land."

Weaving Woman stopped what she was doing and turned to look

at Little Man Wolf.

"That is enough stories for today," she said.

CHAPTER XI

After bringing Little Man Wolf to Weaving Woman and Red Lance, Wrestling Bear left the same evening to return to the McCall farm. Alone, the darkness of the night provided him cover from the watchful eyes of the enemies. He had given instructions to his men to return to Chief Manuelito's camp, and tell him that he would be away for a long time to perform a family duty. At the McCall farm, he would be looking for clues as to what happened to his sister and brother-in-law, and did not want too many braves tramping all over any sign.

He traveled several days and nights before he reached the top of a mountain. He was now deep in Hopi territory. He could feel the raw mountain air brushing against his face as he rode his pony across a wide treeless opening. It was late, and he was not expecting any enemy to be awake to ambush anyone, but Wrestling Bear was by nature a cautious warrior. He listened to every sound. A twig broke when a hare stepped on it as it ran toward its next cover. An owl was hooting up a tree some distance from him. There were a couple of deer moving as quietly as possible in the brush.

Wrestling Bear reached the other side of the opening, and the sweet aroma of pine trees had a quick refreshing effect on him. He remembered the night at the hogan as he sat talking to Weaving Woman and Red Lance. He thought about Smiling Feathers. He had been too preoccupied to think about her. He remembered how she quickly glanced at him when Weaving Woman said she was a beautiful woman, and how she sadly said there were no unmarried men in her village. Now that he was thinking about her, he realized that she was indeed a beautiful woman. Wrestling Bear also remembered how Weaving Woman said to him so many times that he should choose a wife. Smiling Feathers would make a good wife, he thought. But, he knew that he would be away for a long time. She would be married by then. He kicked the side of his pony to make it go faster. He did not want to think about Smiling Feathers anymore.

The McCall farm was still several hills and mountains away. It did not seem that far when he was out hunting with his men. He had been looking forward to bringing Laughing Deer and her family back to Diné Land when he went to see them two years before. He thought she would be very happy to hear about the treaty with General Sherman, and the opportunity to come home in peace. He reminded her that she should live in her homeland, where Changing Woman placed the Diné to live, and where the Navajos could receive the blessings of the Holy People.

"This is my home. I will live where my husband lives," she said, refusing to leave the McCall farm. "We receive blessings from my husband's Holy People."

They had worked hard for four years on that farm, and they were happy. The land was good and fruitful, so Wrestling Bear did not insist. Perhaps he should have, he thought.

Dawn was just breaking when he arrived at the farm. He looked for fresh tracks to see if anybody had been there since they left. There were no new ones. It had not rained since they were there, and the tracks were dry and set in the dirt. There were eleven sets of unshod hooves, and he knew right away those were the tracks he and his braves made. He noted the old tracks of shod horses that milled around in front of the house. From the depth of the tracks he figured there were four heavy men, two light men, and eight average weight men.

"Little Man Wolf said two men were shot off their horses," he thought to himself. Victor McCall would be shooting from the window gun port at the men milling around on their horses in the front yard. He checked the tracks again, and noted that two horses carrying average weight men had reared and dug their hooves into the ground. That would be the two men who were shot off their horses. However, there were no dead bodies in front of the house. The other men could have brought the bodies into the house.

He walked toward to the front of the house. The doorframe was burnt but still standing. From the thickness of the doorframe, Wrestling Bear thought that it would take two heavy men to break down the door. That would be the two heavy men who were first to rush in and get cut down by Victor McCall's Winchester. Even with two big men it would take at least five tries to break down that door. He imagined his brother-in-law shooting from the gun port at the men outside, then turning to the side as the door was finally broken open. Two quick shots killed the two men.

So twelve men had rushed inside the house, including the two who were shot dead as the entered. That left two heavy men, two light ones, and six average weight men. Ten men. Little Man Wolf said two of the men kept shooting at his father who was thrown against the wall with the blast from the guns. These ten men were the ones who hurt Laughing Deer, in the words of Little Man Wolf. Wrestling Bear knew how they were hurting her. She escaped the lust of the blue coat soldiers on the march to Bosque Redondo, only to fall prey to the lust of these evil men. Wrestling Bear looked down as he felt a surge of anger shooting up to his head.

On the ground he saw clumps of ashes and human skulls. He counted six skulls. He could not tell the difference between Laughing Deer, Victor McCall, and the four men that McCall had shot. He did not want to look closer. It would be best to leave things the way they were, lest those men came back to look for the boy.

Wrestling Bear knelt and bowed his head as he softly sang a chant. Then he raised his arms toward the sky. The Coyote had told the Diné when they first entered this Glitter World that death was part of life. The spirit of the dead must move on to the next world. Grieving would interrupt this journey. He was saddened by the deaths of Laughing Deer and Victor McCall, and the chant wished their spirits a safe journey.

When he finished the chant Wrestling Bear dipped his fingers into the ashes and painted his forehead and cheeks. He checked the tracks leading out of the farm. Then he jumped on his horse and rode due west.

CHAPTER XII

"Little Man Wolf, get up!" a loud, stern voice woke him up from a comfortable sleep.

It was Weaving Woman. The harshness of his grandmother's voice surprised him. She had always spoken to him with a soft, loving voice the way Laughing Deer always spoke to him.

"Didn't your mother tell you that if you sleep too much you will wake up with the enemy upon you?"

Lhachaeh, who was sleeping beside him, also woke up.

Little Man Wolf rubbed his eyes and turned but did not get up right away. Then he felt the sting of a whip on his thigh. He jumped up quickly. Lhachaeh started growling.

"Stay!" Little Man Wolf ordered, and Lhachaeh lay down and started whining.

"Go out and greet the dawn!" Weaving Woman said.

He obeyed without saying a word because he was too surprised to say anything. Lhachaeh followed. Outside the hogan the air was chilly with the late autumn wind. He could feel his skin tightening up under his shirt.

"Take off your shirt!" Weaving Woman ordered.

He complied, wondering what he had done to deserve a punishment.

"Run as fast as you can until you reach the foot of that farthest hill. Then come back."

Little Man Wolf started running. Lhachaeh ran beside him. He felt tears welling in his eyes. Then he said to himself, tears are only for women.

It was almost three hours by the time they got back. He was very tired and hungry. His body was drenched with sweat in spite of the cold wind. He felt a little angry with his grandmother because he could not think of anything he did wrong to deserve a punishment that harsh.

As soon as he entered the hogan, his grandmother immediately wrapped a blanket around him and rubbed his body briskly.

"Go and sit by the fire," she said in her usual soft, loving voice. "I will bring your food over." Lhachaeh was already lying down by the fire.

Weaving Woman came over with two plates. One was for the dog.

Smiling Feathers and Little Sunflower came back in from tending the vegetable garden. They went directly to the fire and sat down facing Little Man Wolf.

"The frost did not do much damage," Smiling Feathers said to Weaving Woman.

"That is good."

"I am cold," Little Sunflower said.

"Here. Take the blanket," Little Man Wolf said. "I am not cold anymore."

He stood up and draped the blanket on Smiling Feathers and Little Sunflower.

"Thank you," they both said at the same time.

Little Man Wolf put on his shirt.

"I will check on the horses and sheep," he said as he went out. Lhachaeh walked out behind him.

Early the next morning, Little Man Wolf heard the familiar harsh voice again, "Wake up! Too much sleep will make you weak. You are a warrior. You must be strong, and your mind must be alert. Go out and run!"

In an instant, Little Man Wolf took off his shirt and was out of the door. He did not want to wait for the whip to sting his thigh again. Lhachaeh ran after him. It took them three hours again before they returned, but this time, they had gone farther than the last hill.

Every morning his grandmother woke him up the same way, and always with a reproving comment about the dangers of too much sleep. After about two weeks of this, he woke up by himself, and he and Lhachaeh would be out running toward the hills before dawn. Coming back, he looked forward to Weaving Woman waiting for him with a warm blanket, a brisk rub, and a good breakfast for him and his dog.

Soon he was running every day as a matter of habit, no matter the weather condition or the season.

"You are a warrior. You must be strong, and your mind must be alert," his grandmother's words kept repeating in his mind.

Red Lance was spending more time with him now. He taught Little Man Wolf how to make the bow and arrow, to string and draw, and to aim and shoot at the target. He showed him how to throw the knife, the tomahawk, and the spear, and how to fight with them.

One day, Red Lance was showing him how to grab and hold to subdue the enemy, but every time he did, Little Man Wolf would escape and pin him.

"Where did you learn to wrestle?" Red Lance finally asked.

"It's called *Kung-Fu Wushu*. A Chinese man taught me."

"Where?"

"A mining camp near my father's farm."

"I have never seen those moves. They are very good moves."

Little Man Wolf excelled in everything Red Lance taught him.

"I do not have to teach you how to ride. You already ride well. Your father was a good horseman. He taught you well. But, you must learn to shoot the arrow and throw a tomahawk and a spear on horse back."

He did well on those, too.

Little Man Wolf did not grow much taller as Wrestling Bear had predicted. His body was normal size for a young man of ten, but his legs were not growing as fast. It was no surprise to Little Man Wolf that he was different. He heard what Doctor Kraus said to his father a long time ago, and he understood, even then, that he would be different.

Like all the other Navajo boys, he enjoyed hunting. He could shoot the farthest arrow. He could kill prey with a tomahawk at farther than fifteen feet, fight with a knife or his bare hands, and outwrestle everyone. While he was not the fastest runner among the boys, he could outlast and run the farthest than anyone. It was said that Little Man Wolf could sail in the wind, and go farther than tumbleweed. The other boys looked up to him because he was the only one among them with an Ute scalp hanging on his belt.

One day, he came back to the village riding a very spirited pinto. The story told was that he and Lhachaeh chased the pinto on foot until it could run no more. Then Little Man Wolf jumped on its back and held on to its mane while the mustang pranced, bucked and whirled around and around. The horse even sat down trying to throw the Little Man Wolf off its back. Then it quieted down, and turned its head to look at Little Man Wolf. They were friends after that. No one else could ride the pinto without being thrown. Little Man Wolf named the pinto Running Wind.

CHAPTER XIII

Red Lance decided that it was time for Little Man Wolf to start the other half of his education. Chief Barboncito had grown weak and died the year before, and the people now looked to Chief Manuelito for leadership. There was still hardship, poverty and hunger in Diné Land, and raiding had increased in the search for food. Some young Navajos even raided nearby Mormon settlements and peaceful Mexican villages. Chief Manuelito started to believe that the future of the Navajo nation rested on the white man's education.

Red Lance prepared Little Man Wolf for the change.

"You will live with Padre Tomas and have further education in the ways of the white man. You will obey and respect him, and do whatever he tells you to do. You will continue to practice what you have learned here. You will make your body stronger and your mind alert by running every day before the break of dawn. When Padre Tomas has no need for your services, and he allows you, come home and be with your family."

Padre Tomas made it a point not to talk about his size. He simply kept repeating what he said to the boy when he first came to the village—God loves all his children. He has a purpose and a plan for all of us.

"Jeremiah, when you are here, you will answer to your Christian name when called," Padre Tomas said.

"Yes, Padre Tomas."

The Bible was the only book in the mission, but with its help, Padre Tomas was able to tutor Jeremiah to improve his reading and writing.

"We are ordering more books on literature, mathematics, and history, so you will have a complete education," Padre Tomas promised.

One day, Padre Tomas introduced him to a Navajo boy.

"Jeremiah, this is Henry Chee Dodge. I have been tutoring him. Henry, meet Jeremiah McCall."

They shook hands the white man's way.

The boy was alert, and was always ready with a smile. He spoke English well and was about four years older than Little Man Wolf.

"Are you Navajo?" Jeremiah asked innocently.

"Yes."

"Henry Chee Dodge. That is not Navajo."

"I was born to *Bisnayanchi* of the Coyote Pass People—Jemez clan, and born for Juan Cocinas of the Mexican People. My father worked for the Indian agent Henry Dodge. My father respected Dodge so much he named me after him. Jeremiah McCall is a white man's name. Your hair is yellow and your eyes are blue. Are you really Navajo?"

"My clan calls me Little Man Wolf. I was born to Laughing Deer of the Towering House People Clan, and born for Victor McCall of the Irish People."

Henry Chee Dodge smiled amiably. He was just teasing. Jeremiah liked him immediately.

On Sundays, Jeremiah put on his sacristan vestments and rang the church bell at the belfry. He quickly ran down to the altar, careful to avoid tripping on his oversized vestment, would be ready at the altar to assist Padre Tomas in the mass by the time the worshippers filed in.

The worshippers were mostly tribal women and little children. Some older men would drift in occasionally, but they stayed away to safeguard their image as the brave warrior. While the tribe had not fully accepted the Christian teaching, Padre Tomas was accepted, even respected, as a person. On several occasions, Jeremiah overheard some men, mostly elders, refer to Padre Tomas as a very brave warrior.

After the mass, Jeremiah would carefully put away his vestment, don the deerskin pants that Weaving Woman made for him, and run bare-chested to join Henry Chee Dodge and the Navajo boys up on the hill. Lhachaeh ran after him.

Jeremiah was cleaning in the sacristy one afternoon when he pulled hard at a drawer that was stuck. On the last tug, the whole drawer came loose, and Jeremiah tumbled back. When he regained his balance, he reached inside the drawer casing to see what was stuck. To his surprise, he pulled out a black bandoleer with a pair of shiny six-shooters.

"Padre Tomas, I found these guns in the back of the drawer in the sacristy. Did someone forget them there?" Jeremiah said when he brought the guns to the priest.

"Thank you, my son." That was all Padre Tomas said as he took the guns.

The next time he went home, Little Man Wolf excitedly told Red Lance about the guns that he found. Red Lance smiled and said, "Padre Tomas had not always been a priest."

Little Man Wolf looked at his grandfather trying to understand what he meant.

"He was a *pistolero*—a very brave warrior. Long before your mother was born, Padre Tomas came to the valley alone. He wore those pistols in the bandoleer and was following the trail of Mexican bandits who had taken his wife from their ranch up north. He caught up with them near the Nevada border, and killed all six of them. The bandits had been torturing his wife and taking turns doing bad things to her. She did not even recognize her own husband. She had completely lost her mind. Thomas wrapped a blanket around her and cleaned her body to prepare her for the long trip across the prairie to their home. One night, Thomas woke up and found her gone.

He searched for her all night, calling her name. He did not care if there were enemies around, and whether they heard him or not. He was desperate to find his wife. The following morning he found her sitting against a boulder. She was dead. She had slit her own throat with his knife."

Little Man Wolf did not say a word. The images of his mother and father, their burning house, and the hooded men kept intruding in his mind. It had been awhile since he thought about that night. But now, remembering it made him feel disquieted.

"I found Thomas unconscious in the desert," Red Lance continued. "He must have been wandering for days with no food and water. His horse did not leave him. It just stood there looking weak for lack of water, but patiently waiting for its master to get up. I brought Thomas to our hogan. He was delirious and kept calling out his wife's name. It must have been four weeks before he was well enough to understand what had happened. He lived with us for about a year and even learned to speak like a Navajo. One day, I got a report that a band of Mexican bandits had raided a village and took some captives. As I prepared to leave with my band, Thomas asked my permission to come along. We sighted the bandits, and there must have been a hundred of them. I had twenty warriors with me. The bandits were walking their horses slowly. The captives were tied together and attached to a long a rope. I ordered to attack. Thomas was the first to reach them, killing five bandits almost immediately. He kept on killing like a cougar killing sheep. The surprised Mexicans did not have time to prepare, but they killed two of my men. We killed all of them, and took plenty of scalps. We returned to the village with fifty saved captives and over a hundred sheep. That night the whole clan celebrated the brave warriors. A special honor was given to Thomas for the most kills. He left us shortly after that, and went on hunting slave traders on his own. Years later, he came back as a priest. He was now a man of peace."

CHAPTER XIV

After Jeremiah discovered the six-shooters in the sacristy, he tried almost daily to persuade the old priest to teach him how to use guns. He argued that this was part of his education. He said that he was already skillful with the bow and arrow, spear, knife and tomahawk and knowing how to use the white man's weapons would complete his education in weaponry.

"But, you are only ten years old," Padre Tomas pointed out.

"I have already killed an enemy. An Ute scalp hangs in my belt."

Jeremiah was surprised with himself after he said that. He sounded the way a proud Navajo warrior would speak in a war council. He had never spoken that way before. He meant no disrespect toward Padre Tomas, and he felt embarrassed thinking he had done so.

Padre Tomas listened patiently, but he knew what was in Jeremiah's heart. He knew that Little Man Wolf, the warrior, would soon dominate Jeremiah's personality. He could sense that it was seething underneath, and would soon cry out for revenge. He understood it too well, having been there, and knew that with all his Christian teachings the rage would still surface, and had to be satisfied. He felt that he had a responsibility toward the boy, that if and when it happened, Jeremiah should not fail for lack of preparation.

"Let's ride up to the mountain," Padre Tomas said.

Jeremiah watched as Padre Tomas strapped on the bandoleer

and checked the guns. Then, with lightning speed, he pulled out one gun, cocked and shot repeatedly until it was empty. Then he holstered it and simultaneously pulled out the other gun, cocked and shot repeatedly again until it was empty. With a twirl of his finger, he slid it back in the holster. All this happened in the blink of an eye.

Jeremiah was unable to say anything. The loud explosions of the guns were still ringing in his ears. The graceful way Padre Tomas handled the guns was still in his mind's eye. "Padre, I have never seen such shooting!"

"This is a Colt single action six-shooter. You pull back the hammer as you draw, then point it and shoot. You have to pull the hammer back before each shot. Practice that until you can pull the hammer back, point and shoot in one movement. Remember, the first shot is the most important. You may not get a second shot if you are slow, or you miss."

Jeremiah put on the bandoleer and tried to do it the way Padre Tomas did it, but he was slow and awkward. After several tries, Padre Tomas stopped him.

"These guns are not the right guns for you," father Tomas said. "The barrels are too long, and will take longer to clear the holster. A 4-inch barrel would be more practical. The Winchester is also too long. You need a carbine, which has a 15-inch barrel length, instead of this standard 24-inch for the rifle. The carbine is an excellent saddle rifle. It is easier to pull out and shoot while riding. You may lose some accuracy at a distance, but for what you want to do, it would be fine. You don't intend to shoot someone standing 500 yards from you. But, we have time. We'll see what we can find for you when you get older. In the meantime, you can practice with these."

Whenever they had a chance, Padre Tomas and Jeremiah rode up to the mountains, and spent hours and hours practicing with the six-shooters, the rifle and the shotgun. Padre Tomas showed him where to position himself in a shootout, how to read the opponent's movements, how to draw fast and where to shoot if killing was unavoidable.

What Jeremiah lacked in speed, he made up in accuracy. He always hit what he was aiming at. Soon, he developed a high sensitivity to movement and noise so that he could hit a target with his eyes closed by listening to the swirling of the wind around his target.

"How do you do that?" Padre Tomas asked, amazed.

"I don't know Padre, I just do it."

"You have a gift."

Jeremiah remembered how Lee Bok blindfolded them when they practiced *Kung-Fu Wushu*. He told them to detect the position of the opponent, and attack when they sensed his presence. Listen to the wind, Lee Bok would say. Listen to the wind.

As Jeremiah got older and stronger, he developed better control. With constant practice, he was finally able to draw, pull the hammer and shoot with lightning speed.

"If we get the right guns, no one will ever get the better of you," Padre Tomas said.

At the age of fourteen, Little Man Wolf had a body as hard as a rock. He walked about with a bearing that exuded self-confidence and determination. His peers regarded him as they would regard a true headman. His education, too, with Padre Tomas was going well. Being around Henry Chee Dodge, who was a bright student, also helped because they inspired and challenged each other to learn.

The summer sun threw scorching heat on the ground that afternoon as they returned from their daily shooting practice up in the mountain. There seemed to be some commotion going on in the village. There were about thirty Navajo men on horseback wearing some kind of uniform. Jeremiah immediately noticed the man in front. He was the biggest Navajo he had ever seen. He was well over six feet tall, with a very imposing bearing.

"It's Chief Manuelito," Padre Tomas said.

Chief Manuelito immediately recognized the priest. "Greetings, Padre Tomas."

"Greetings, Chief Manuelito. To what do we owe this welcome visit?"

"My Navajo police force and I are chasing Mexican Bandits that raided one of our villages and took many captives. They have many men and guns. We need more men to join us. Who is this young man with the golden hair?"

"That is Little Man Wolf, my grandson," Red Lance said. He was standing among those in the crowd.

"Yes, the young warrior who killed an Ute brave with a tomahawk. My men, who were with Wrestling Bear, told me. I see he is older now. You will join us Little Man Wolf."

"It will be an honor Chief Manuelito," Little Man Wolf said, looking at Red Lance who nodded in agreement. Little Man Wolf was very happy for being called a warrior by Chief Manuelito, and to be invited to join the pursuit.

"Take the six-shooters and the Winchester," Padre Tomas said. "You have enough cartridge in the bandoleer."

"Thank you, Padre," Little Man Wolf said.

"Vaya con Dios."

"Take these too, Little Man Wolf." Red Lance said handing him a bow and a quiver of arrows.

"Thank you, Grandfather,"

"Do well, my son."

"Has Wrestling Bear returned yet?" Chief Manuelito asked Red Lance

"Not yet, Chief."

"He would be good to have in this fight. You too, Red Lance and Padre Tomas, if time had not passed for the warriors in you."

"Yes. Time has passed," Padre Tomas agreed.

"Let the young men take their place in glory," Red Lance said.

Twenty other young men rode up to join. Henry Chee Dodge was among them. He nodded and smiled at Little Man Wolf, who nodded and smiled back.

"We must go now before the bandits make it to the border," Chief

Manuelito said.

They rode away in a cloud of dust. Lhachaeh also ran, keeping pace beside Running Wind.

CHAPTER XV

Chief Manuelito and his band found the Mexican bandits two weeks later. They were camped by the Colorado River at the Grand Canyon. Little Man Wolf went out with the scouts. With his small stature and agility, he was able to get closer than the rest without being detected. He reported back to Chief Manuelito that there were close to two hundred bandits, heavily armed with six-shooters and rifles, and some with machetes. They were spread out along the riverbank in groups of six to ten people. There was a celebration going on all over the camp. There were singing, music and loud laughter. Some drunken men were shooting their guns in the air. About one hundred captive women and children were seated at the middle of the camp with four men standing guard. Little Man Wolf could hear women crying and screaming and he saw women being dragged away from the group, and raped behind the trees. The horses were not tethered all together, but banded close to each group of men.

Chief Manuelito knew that a frontal attack, even with the advantage of a surprise, would result in many deaths for his men and the captives. He needed to pare down the enemy force before they could expose themselves. Also, when they were ready to attack, the bandits should be kept away from their horses to prevent their escape.

He assigned one man for each band of horses. On his signal they were to cut the rope binding the horses and run them off. Then he chose the strongest warriors to crawl with their knives and pick off any bandit who separated from their group.

"Chief Manuelito, I want to go," Little Man Wolf said in a low voice when he was not chosen.

"These are big and strong men. They are too big for young warriors like you," Chief Manuelito said as softly as possible. The wind could carry the sound to the enemy camp.

"I am not afraid of them."

"You are brave but bravery is not enough."

"I have wrestled men as big as a bear and defeated them."

Chief Manuelito thought for a while. He had not the time to argue with this headstrong young man.

"Go then and prove yourself! Be very quiet."

"Thank you!" Then to Henry Chee Dodge, "Please keep my guns and bow. I will be back for them later,"

"Little Man Wolf," Henry Chee Dodge said as he took the weapons, "Be careful."

"I will," Little Man Wolf replied, as he unsheathed his Bowie knife.

"Lhachaeh, stay." The dog whined, but lay down and obeyed.

Little Man Wolf crawled to the edge of the tree grove. There he could watch the enemy camp a few yards away toward the river. He heard a soft muffled cry of a woman, and the grunting of a man. He crawled quietly toward the sound. As he expected, a woman was being raped by one of the bandits. In one quick move, Little Man Wolf grabbed the man's neck, slit his throat, and covered the mouth of the surprised woman to stop her from screaming. The bandit's blood spilled on the woman's face. He whispered something to the woman in Navajo, and pointed her in the direction where Chief Manuelito was waiting. After she left, Little Man Wolf took the scalp of the Mexican bandit and crawled quietly to the other side.

Little Man Wolf was away for a long while. When he returned, there were six women huddled near Henry Chee Dodge and Lhachaeh. They were the six that he had saved and sent to Chief Manuelito. Little Man Wolf also had six new scalps on his belt.

Chief Manuelito greeted Little Man Wolf with a nod and a smile.

A few minutes later the other warriors returned with scalps on their belts.

"That is good," Chief Manuelito said. "Now we attack."

"Chief Manuelito, Chee Dodge and I can take care of the four men guarding the captives," Little Man Wolf said. "We can do it quietly with bow and arrow. Then we can move the captives to safety before you attack."

"Your plan is good, Little Man Wolf," Chief Manuelito said. "We will do so."

Chief Manuelito ordered the warriors to the edge of tree grove. Little Man Wolf and Henry Chee Dodge positioned themselves where they had a clear path for their arrows. Their plan was to shoot two arrows each, one after the other, to take out the four guards. Then, Henry Chee Dodge would run in and lead the captives to safety, as Chief Manuelito and his band, including Little Man Wolf, attacked.

The night was filled with yelling and screaming, gunshots echoing back from all over the canyon and the swishing sound of arrows as they flew in the air. Horses were galloping in all directions. Some Mexican bandits ran to the river to escape, trying to swim away, only to drown as they were shot down.

"*Navajo Blanco*?" some Mexicans incredulously said as Little Man Wolf shot them down. They could not believe there was a white warrior among the Navajo fighting even more fiercely than the other warriors.

"*Hijo de puta!*" some pointed and cursed at him as they lay dying.

The fighting lasted for only a few minutes, but hundreds lay dead in the sand. It was possible some bandits were able to escape in the dark. None of the captives were hurt in the fighting, but five Navajo warriors lay dead. Little Man Wolf went to check them one by one. Henry Chee Dodge was not one of them. Then he went around to look for his friend. Lhachaeh followed wherever Little Man Wolf went. Little Man Wolf met Chief Manuelito who was standing quietly in the middle of the carnage.

"Your friend is not hurt. He is there, taking care of the captives," Chief Manuelito said. "Little Man Wolf, you both did well."

"*Ahéhee*. Thank you."

It took several days to reach the village at Fort Defiance. Some of the captives were not well and could not move fast. They were immediately distributed among the families to be cared for and healed of their wounds.

That night there was a celebration at the village. There was singing, dancing, and drum beating to thank the Holy People.

The young U.S. soldiers who were standing guard at the fort became nervous with the sound of the Navajos drums and chants.

"What is going on with those redskins?" they asked each other.

"Are they turning hostile?"

"Ask the sergeant," one young recruit suggested.

"I don't know," the sergeant said. "They are not supposed to be hostile. Stay alert, though, in case they attack."

A captain came up to the rampart to look.

"Captain Murphy, what is going on?"

"I don't know, but I'll find out. Sergeant, have my horse saddled and ready."

"Sir, are you going out there?"

"That's the best way to find out, isn't it?"

"Yes, sir. I'll have your horse ready."

Captain Thomas Murphy rode out from the fort directly to the center of the village. The warriors who were huddled around the bonfire stepped aside to let him pass.

"Greetings, Chief Manuelito."

"Greetings Captain Murphy. You are welcome to sit with us."

Captain Murphy dismounted and walked with his horse to Chief Manuelito.

"May I ask what the celebration is all about?"

"We are giving thanks to the Holy People for saving our women and children from the Mexican bandits. We are also honoring the brave warriors who saved them."

"I see."

"I remember you," Little Man Wolf stood up and said.

Captain Murphy looked at the short young warrior with a golden hair. The warrior was obviously a white man.

"You are the man who saved my mother from those soldiers who wanted to hurt her at Canyon de Chelly."

"This is Little Man Wolf, one of my brave warriors," Chief Manuelito said.

Captain Murphy hesitated for a while. Then he remembered the night Colonel Kit Carson rounded all the Navajos at Canyon de Chelly. He remembered the woman who had a little boy with golden hair.

"You are the little boy with the golden hair?" Captain Murphy asked.

"Yes, Captain. My father meant to thank you."

"Where are your parents now? Are they here?" He looked around but saw no white man, except for Padre Tomas, whom he recognized. He nodded a greeting toward Padre Tomas, who acknowledged it.

"My parents passed on, Captain."

"I'm sorry to hear that." He sensed that it would not be good to ask how they died.

"You are welcome to stay and celebrate with us," Chief Manuelito offered.

"It's best that I get back to my men. They wanted to know what the celebration is all about. Chief Manuelito, your Navajo police force has done good work. I will report it to the General."

"I send my greetings to the general," Chief Manuelito said.

A Shaman presided over the rites of the Enemy Way. There was story telling about the bravery of the Navajo warriors. They honored the warriors, Little Man Wolf in particular, who had the most kills. Fifteen Mexican scalps hung on his belt.

Red Lance sat proudly, listening to the stories. Padre Tomas sat beside him. Weaving Woman, Smiling Feathers and Little Sunflower sat with the women, also listening. Little Sunflower was smiling to herself, feeling that by honoring Little Man Wolf, she too was being honored. At the age of twelve, she had blossomed into a very beautiful young woman like her sister. She was also beginning to have the feelings of a woman. She had grown up with Little Man Wolf, and in her mind, the Holy People had ordained it. Little Man Wolf was her brave warrior. He was the bravest among all of them, and he belonged to her.

CHAPTER XVI

Life at Diné Land was beginning to settle down to a peaceful existence. It was very rare that Mexican bandits, the Ute or Hopi tribes would venture to raid any of the Navajo villages to steal livestock or take captives for slavery. If they did, the Navajo police force immediately took care of them. Chief Manuelito also stopped the Navajo braves from raiding Mormon settlements and peaceful Mexican villages. The United States military did the best they could to live up to their part of the treaty of 1868 between the Navajo chiefs and General William Tecumseh Sherman. But, their attention was mostly diverted to troubles with Apache Chief Victorio and his raiders.

More lands were slowly being returned to the Navajo people by the United States government, and the yield on the land was beginning to look more and more promising. The livestock had also grown to thousands of sheep and hundreds of cattle.

Little Man Wolf was still doing his daily run at dawn with Lhachaeh, and the sessions on the hill with Padre Tomas. Gun practice was more like a sport with them now, and not like earlier days with its underlying sordid purpose. Red Lance also welcomed the company of Little Man Wolf when he went spear fishing, which had become his sole passion in his old age.

Little Sunflower was growing more beautiful every day, and young braves had been coming around more, showing off their skills whenever they thought Little Sunflower was watching. On her part, she never paid attention to any of them. She concentrated on seeing to the needs of Little Man Wolf. They had grown very close as they grew up, and with no words spoken, they both felt they were promised to each other. She was now a few inches taller than Little Man Wolf, but it was no matter. She loved his beautiful face, and as a warrior, none was more skillful and braver than Little Man Wolf.

It had been seven years since Little Man Wolf last saw Wrestling Bear. His tired horse brought him in one morning. He was dehydrated and half-dead from festering wounds. Little Man Wolf took Wrestling Bear off the horse, and carried him inside the hogan.

"Little Sunflower," Little Man Wolf called. "Water the horse and feed it. Then go find Red Lance."

Smiling Feathers immediately wrapped Wrestling Bear in a blanket as Weaving Woman grabbed her medicine pouch and prepared some herbs and sacred stones to tend to his wounds.

Wrestling Bear was much older than Little Man Wolf remembered.

Soon the shaman arrived with Red Lance. Little Sunflower told him that Wrestling Bear came home wounded and gravely ill.

When they went inside the hogan, Smiling Feathers was sitting beside Wrestling Bear, grieving.

"Are you his woman?" the shaman asked.

Smiling Feathers nodded, but did not say a word.

"Take off your clothes and lie beside him. Keep him warm."

Smiling Feathers looked at Weaving Woman who nodded approval. She went inside the blanket, took off her clothes and lay beside Wrestling Bear.

"Go get some more firewood," the shaman ordered Little Sunflower.

The shaman started singing the Enemy Way songs. For three days and three nights, the drums beat, the women wailed, and the men danced to drive away the evil spirit. Padre Tomas prayed, but did not interfere with the ritual.

From the half-delirious Wrestling Bear, Little Man Wolf was

able to get part of the story of what happened to him. Wrestling Bear had gone back to the McCall farm to gather clues about that night. He pieced together the story Little Man Wolf told him with the tracks left by the raiders. There were a total of fourteen men. Four were killed. The ten surviving raiders left the McCall farm and rode west for about twenty miles, and then camped for the night. In the morning they split up in three directions. Three average size men went west. One heavy man and one skinny one went south toward Mexico and the others went east to New Mexico, and maybe Texas.

For two years, Wrestling Bear followed the tracks of the three men who went west, crossing mountains and rivers. He avoided the white men's towns, and where the tracks disappeared he would talk to some friendly tribes for some lead.

On a mountain trail, he met some Cocopah tribesmen, who called themselves *Xawil Kunyavaei*, Those Who Live On The River. They were the known enemies of the Yuma tribe, but they had no quarrel with Navajo. The tribesmen worked hauling logs from the mountains to Port Famine on the edge of the Colorado River. The tribesmen knew of one of the men that Wrestling Bear described. He lived on the riverboat, and worked as a gambler.

"White gambler is evil man. He looks at Cocopah with hatred in his eyes. Other white men do not like him. They say he cheats at cards and steals their money," one tribesman said.

The Cocopah had one of their members working as navigator on board the paddle-wheel steamboat. Disguising Wrestling Bear as one of them, the Cocopah navigator arranged for him to work on board the steamboat. Wrestling Bear left his horse with the tribesmen who promised to take care of it until he returned. As the steamboat traveled downriver to Port Yuma, Wrestling Bear found the gambler, followed him to his room, and with harsh persuasion, extracted all the names of the other nine raiders who were with him at the McCall farm. He left the man dead with a slit throat and a derringer bullet wound in his chest. He took the man's money to make it look like a robbery. Wrestling Bear arranged the clues to point to any of the other steamboat gamblers the man might have cheated.

When the boat reached Yuma, Wrestling Bear helped unload the cargo, and then quietly disappeared with the passenger crowd. He went back to the tribesmen, and gave them the money he took from the gambler. They did not want any payment, until they were told that the money came from the man who hated them and they hated in return.

That was all that Little Man Wolf could get until Wrestling Bear fully recovered and collected his thoughts.

"How is he?" Little Man Wolf asked Smiling Feathers.

"Still not well."

The following morning he asked again as soon as he and Lhachaeh came back from their early dawn run. The answer was the same.

Little Sunflower watched Little Man Wolf and tried to calm him down.

"You must be patient," she said. "Wrestling Bear will soon be well."

Little Man Wolf knew that even if Wrestling Bear recovered, he would no longer be fit to take up the hunt again. He needed to know what happened to the other nine men. He knew that it would be up to him now to finish the task of avenging his parents. Every day that Wrestling Bear had not recovered, Little Man Wolf would get more and more restless.

"Padre Tomas what must I do?" he asked the priest.

"What does your heart say, Jeremiah?"

"There is darkness in my heart, Padre Tomas."

"There are forces within you telling you what to do."

"In all these years, I thought I had forgiven."

"And have you?"

"There is fire within that is consuming me. I see my father blown to the wall. I see my mother being stripped naked and men, one after the other, hurting her."

Padre Tomas did not say anything. The image of his own wife

being tortured and raped by bandits had once more took hold of his entire being.

"Jeremiah, please go to the chapel and pray. You may find peace in there."

Henry Chee Dodge came to see Little Man Wolf.

"Where is he, Padre?"

"He is in the chapel."

Henry Chee Dodge went to the chapel and saw Little Man Wolf on his knees. He approached quietly not wanting to disturb his prayer.

"Chee, my soul is in turmoil. I thought I had done enough killing in my life," Little Man Wolf said, turning to look at his friend.

"I heard about Wrestling Bear. I am sorry he is hurt."

"Padre Tomas told me to pray for guidance."

"Do you want me to stay here with you?"

"I have to pray alone, Chee."

"I will go. Call me if you if you need me. I will go with you whatever you want to do."

"You are my true friend, Chee."

Little Man Wolf spent the night in the chapel praying. At dawn, he left with Lhachaeh and Running Wind for their daily run. When he came back, he went directly to Padre Tomas.

"I prayed the whole night to seek guidance and peace for my own soul. In my mind I saw the spirits of my mother and father. For seven years their spirits have been wandering. They are lost. They cannot finish their journey to the next world until their deaths are avenged."

"Jeremiah, you are a Christian now. You understand the power of prayer."

"I am Little Man Wolf. I am a Navajo warrior."

Wrestling Bear was much better now. He told Little Man Wolf that it took more years, but he finally tracked down and killed the other two men he was chasing. When he found them, they were with five other men who had nothing to do with the deaths of Laughing

Deer and Victor McCall. He had to kill three of the others to get to the men he was after. He was wounded, but he got away. That was all he remembered. His horse must have traveled almost a hundred miles to get home.

"There are seven other men that I still have to track down. My wounds are healing. I will be able to travel again in a week."

"Wrestling Bear your work is done. It is now my turn," Little Man Wolf said.

"I have not completed my work. I am not finished."

"You have done well, my son," Red Lance spoke. "Little Man Wolf has already proven himself a mighty warrior. Give him the honor by letting him fulfill his duty."

Wrestling Bear was quiet. He had not expected this, but he understood that it was right. He gave Little Man Wolf the names of the seven men, and where they might be found.

Little Sunflower was there, too, to listen to the story. When Little Man Wolf stood up, she asked, "Will you be going away then?"

"I must."

"I know."

"Go to the smokehouse and prepare yourself. I will get the shaman," Red Lance said.

The smokehouse ritual was to cleanse and purify the body of a warrior who was going away from the blessed land to undertake an important task. It was also to seek blessing and protection of the Holy People so that no harm would come to him in his journey.

That night Padre Tomas came to visit Little Man Wolf.

"I brought some gifts that you will need on your journey," Padre Tomas said.

He opened the blanket he was carrying and laid out the gifts.

There was a brand new black leather bandoleer, two Colt .44-40 caliber double-action revolvers, and a Winchester '73 carbine.

"The Colt revolvers have 4" barrels for a quicker draw. They will clear the holsters faster. The guns are double-action, so there is no need to pull back the hammer before shooting. Just pull the trigger and shoot. The Winchester has a 15" barrel and is easier to pull out from the saddle and shoot than the standard 24". Both the Colt and the Winchester shoot the same 44-caliber cartridge, so you don't have to carry two kinds. These are the guns I promised to get you when you were ready. It is time I give them to you. May God be with you, my son."

"Padre Tomas, I don't know how to thank you."

"You can thank me by remembering everything I taught you. Come home safe."

The following morning before dawn, Little Man Wolf quietly put on his bandoleer with the two Colt six-shooters, grabbed his tomahawk, Bowie knife and Winchester and went out of the hogan. Lhachaeh followed. Running Wind, who had been waiting outside all night, walked slowly toward him. Little Man Wolf breathed in the cool air, and looked around.

There was a slight rustle behind him. He turned around to see Little Sunflower.

"I prepared this for your journey," she said handing him a pouch of food.

"I will be away for a long time," Little Man Wolf said.

"I will be here when you return."

They held each other's hands for a long time, and looked into each other's eyes. Then they embraced.

Running Wind sat on the ground and Little Man Wolf got on its back. The horse stood up and walked slowly away from the village. Lhachaeh walked beside it.

"Tell Chee Dodge that this is something I must do myself."

Little Sunflower stood there for a very long time, following them with her eyes until they reached the farthest hill. The sun was beginning to chase the darkness away.

CHAPTER XVII

Little Man Wolf woke up to the sound of a rattlesnake and Lhachaeh growling. Running Wind was stomping its hoof on the ground. The rattling sound came from near the huge boulder about thirty feet away.

"Whoa, boys. I know. The snake is not coming over for a visit."

The snake was just letting them know that it was there, he thought. It did not have any intention of slithering toward them. Besides, Running Wind would just stomp it to death, or Lhachaeh would tear its neck out.

Little Man Wolf thought it interesting how the animals signaled to each other. It seemed to show some respect for each other. Each one was dangerous enough to kill the other, and yet they opted for peace, so long as the other respected its right to live.

The sun was just about ready to show its face over the horizon. The air was nippy, and Little Man Wolf decided to add more wood to the fire that was on its last dying ember.

He stood up and stretched, reaching up as high as he could. A hawk was already out on the prowl in the sky. A coyote was howling away the last vestiges of the night. Somewhere in the half-darkness, creatures were scampering away for safety.

As he did every morning when he got up, he checked his six-shooters, strapped on his bandoleer, and set up tin cans and bottles for target practice. Today, he set them up on top of a rock by the river, away from the rattlesnake. He stood facing the sun, which had now banished the darkness. Padre Tomas taught him to practice while the sun shone directly behind the target.

"But the sun blinds me. I can't see the targets," he had objected.

"That is precisely the point, my son," Padre Tomas said. "You don't always have a choice where you stand when somebody calls you out. The one calling you out has first choice. He will always position himself with the sun toward his back and you will have to shoot with the sun in your eyes."

He turned and walked about twenty paces while keeping his mind focused on the targets behind him. Then, with a quick turn and draw of his guns, Little Man Wolf shot two tins cans into the air, shot them again three more times while they were still up in the air, and then twice more before they landed on the ground. The sound of the guns thundered through the valley and echoed back like a cannon. With a twirl and a twist, he stuck the guns back into the bandoleer. He pulled them out again and reloaded.

The dog started growling and sniffing the air.

"I see him Lhachaeh," he said quietly without raising his head.

High up on the hill behind him was a man on a horse watching them. The distance was out of range for a six-shooter, but Little Man Wolf noted that the man's rifle was still strapped on the side of his saddle.

He could not see who it was, but could tell the man was not planning to shoot. Perhaps the rider was just curious, he thought.

When he looked up toward the hill, the man was gone. He moves fast, Little Man Wolf thought.

Before he could go back to his target shooting, the man appeared from around the trail on the side of the mountain with his horse walking lazily toward Little Man Wolf.

"That wuz some fine shootin' you did. I've never seen anythin' like it befor'. I was watchin' from up the hill."

"I saw you. You were up there for awhile."

"Yes, I was. It was fascinating to watch."

The man was about the same age as Little Man Wolf, perhaps a few years older. He had blue eyes, high cheekbones, large front teeth, and a smile that was half-amused and half a sneer. He wore suspenders, with a six-shooter stuck in his waist, and a crumpled shirt and scarf that looked liked they had never seen water and soap. He also wore a funny looking hat with a green band.

Little Man Wolf sensed that the man was not there to harm him. Even the dog stopped growling, and started rolling on the ground to entertain itself unmindful of the visitor.

"I can't place the accent. Are you from these parts?" Little Man Wolf asked.

"Don't mind the accent, I have several. Actually, I'm from New York City. Mom and I moved to Silver City, New Mexico when dad died. She died five years ago. Name's William Bonney. Call me Billy," he said pleasantly, extending his hand.

"Jeremiah McCall. Call me Little Man Wolf,"

"I think I know you. You're the one Mexicans call *Navajo Blanco*—White Navajo."

"Perhaps. Different people call me different names. But I know you. You're the one they call Billy the Kid."

"I've been called the kid because of my age. You look like about my age yourself. Maybe younger?"

"Sixteen. I was just getting ready to have breakfast. You care to join me for some hard-boiled eggs and beef jerky? Too early to fish."

"Yes, thank you. That's very kind."

"Sorry I don't have any coffee, though. I don't even have a coffee pot. Too big and too noisy to carry around."

"I have one. An old prospector gave it me. Gave me coffee beans, too."

After a quiet breakfast the man called Billy said, "That was a fine breakfast. Kinda wakes you up. Been ridin' all night. Thanks again."

"You're welcome."

"If you don't mind my asking, what are you doin' out here on the range by yourself?"

"Going north."

"Santa Fe?"

"Yes, maybe as far as Kansas."

"Dodge City?"

"Maybe."

"You're going after the men who killed your folks."

Little Man Wolf paused and stared at Billy.

"I heard about the men you killed at Betsy's Saloon in Nogales. Jesse Fremont and Tom Baxter. Tough, wild *Hombre*s. Used to ride with an old enemy of mind, Curly Bill Brosius, and his boss Johnny Ringo."

Little Man Wolf said nothing. He did not want to talk about it.

"I also heard about the eighteen bandits you killed two years ago."

"Fifteen."

"The Mexicans talk about it. They say *Navajo Blanco*, who the Injuns call *Pequeño Hombre Lobo,* killed all the bandidos by himself."

"I was with Navajo Chief Manuelito. I did not kill all of them. There were around two hundred bandits."

"Fifteen bandits—you killed fifteen bandits. If you're sixteen now, that makes you fourteen then. That is really something."

Little Man Wolf said nothing. He did not want to encourage the conversation on that subject.

"*Hombre*, I have a lot of respect for you."

Little Man Wolf still did not say anything.

"Listen, Jeremiah."

"Little Man Wolf."

"Little Man Wolf. I would like to do some target shooting with you before I go. Do you mind?"

"That would be alright. I'm not quite done myself."

They spent a good part of the morning shooting tin cans, bottles, wood, pebbles and anything they could throw up in the air and shoot. Each time they did they became more relaxed with each other's presence. They also developed respect for each other's ability and skill in handling guns. More and more they just became two young men having fun and losing themselves, as they would have when they were young boys, to some forgotten childhood game.

"That's really some guns you have Little Man Wolf. What are they?"

"Colt .44-40 double-action with 4-inch barrel. Clears the holster quickly."

"Cartridge is the same as the Winchester '73?"

"Right. Makes it easy to have just one type cartridge."

All of a sudden two shots rang out. Two men were galloping fast toward them, shooting their guns. Almost simultaneously, Little Man Wolf and Billy quickly got out two shots each bringing down the two men, their horses tumbling down in front of them.

Another man was galloping toward them from behind. He had his gun drawn. Little Man Wolf brought him down.

A man on the ridge started shooting at them with a rifle, letting out one shot after another, and pinning them down. He was out of range for the six-shooters.

Running Wind started to move toward Little Man Wolf, sensing that he needed the Winchester strapped to the saddle.

"Stay!" Little Man Wolf commanded. He was concerned the gunman might shoot his horse. "Lhachaeh, get up there."

The dog crept on the side, out of the man's view from the ridge. Then it ran up the trail on the side of the mountain.

Moments later, Little Man Wolf and Billy heard the man screaming as he fell off his horse and down the side of the mountain.

"Golly, that's some dog you've got, Little Man Wolf," Billy said.

"He helps."

"What's its name?"

"Lhachaeh."

"Lhachaeh. Does it mean anything?"

"It means dog."

"And your horse. It's smart, too."

"That's Running Wind."

Little Man Wolf turned his attention to the three dead men.

"I don't know these boys. Who are they Billy?"

"Bounty hunters. They have been dogging my trail for three days now."

"Any more of them?"

"Not for now. At least, not from this bunch."

"Who then?"

"There is a posse led by a man named Dolan from Lincoln County."

"The Lincoln County Cattle War?"

"Yes. I was involved in that. I'm one of The Regulators with Alexander McSween. You know the story. They have been writing about it in the papers."

"Your group killed Sheriff William Brady and his deputy, and they killed McSween, your employer."

"Brady was working for Dolan. They started the war by killing John Tunstall, McSween's partner. Dolan had hired killers like Curly Bill Brosius."

"Now, it's out of hand. I heard the U.S. Cavalry is also looking for you."

"They won't find me."

"Where are you bound for?" Little Man Wolf asked.

"I'm goin' to Mexico. But first I have to see my friend Doc Scurlock in Tascosa, Texas. Any chance you might be going to Mexico?"

"Might. Perhaps later."

"Maybe I'll run into you again."

"Be a pleasure."

"Hope to see you in Mexico. Don't stay here too long."

"Watch yourself Billy."

"You too, Little Man Wolf."

"You bet."

CHAPTER XVIII

Running Wind whirled around sensing that Lhachaeh had found some tracks. Little Man Wolf, the pinto and the dog seemed to have their own quiet signals. No sounds or words need always be given or spoken.

Little Man Wolf jumped off the pinto and inspected the tracks. They were about four hours old. The horse that made the tracks was carrying an average-size man. The impression on the ground showed that one shoe nail was bent out of shape. The horse was limping, and must be in pain. It would be walking slowly. The rider would need a blacksmith and the nearest town was Laguna, fifteen miles away.

Little Man Wolf looked at the horizon. It would be dark in about an hour. He will have to ride part of the way in pitch darkness, relying on Running Wind's instincts to find the way.

When he reached the town, the blacksmith was just about to close for the night.

"I'm closed, son, I just shut down the furnace. I don't normally work this late. I just did a man a favor, feeling sorry for his horse."

The blacksmith kept looking at Lhachaeh as he spoke.

"That animal of yours, is it a wolf?"

"Could be part wolf. I never asked."

"It looks mean."

"He's okay. Is that his horse?"

"Yes, that's it. Had a shoe nail all bent and sticking out on the side."

"That belongs to my friend. Name's JB."

"Yep. That's him alright—sez so on his saddle. Pardon my saying, but your friend is not very nice to his animal. Rode him even when he knew the horse was limping."

"Where is he right now?"

"Went to the saloon down the street."

"Can you water and feed my horse?"

"Sure can."

"I may leave before dawn. Can you leave my horse in the outside corral so I don't bother waking you?"

"Will do."

Little Man Wolf jumped off Running Wind. The blacksmith looked at him curiously.

"Don't mean no offense, son, but you are the smallest man I've seen."

"No offense taken."

The blacksmith took the reins of the pinto.

"Why, this is an Injun horse. Unshod, is it? You're no Injun. Where'd you get it?"

Little Man Wolf flipped a silver dollar over to the man.

"I'll be at the saloon."

Little Man Wolf pushed the swinging door to the saloon carefully. The place looked like any other saloon he had seen. There were men drinking at the bar, women sitting and laughing with some men. A group of men at one corner were playing poker, and there was a fat lady among them who had the most number of chips in front of her.

"Lhachaeh, stay," he said softly.

Everybody looked at him as he entered. They had never seen a little man before. A few of the women giggled, and whispered to each other. After a few moments, the novelty about him waned, and the people all went back to whatever they were doing. Little Man Wolf went over to the nearest empty table and sat down. A woman came over.

"What'll you have?"

"Beer."

She left and came back with a mug of beer. Little Man Wolf put a silver dollar on the table.

"This is all I'm going to have. You may keep the change."

"Thanks."

Little Man Wolf looked around. He carefully observed what everyone was doing. He did not see anybody who might be JB. A woman and a man were going up the stairs. He watched them as they staggered up step by step. A door upstairs opened, and a woman came out. She looked down in the direction of Little Man Wolf, and then went back inside the room. The door opened again, but this time just a crack. Somebody was peering from behind the door. When the door closed again, Little Man Wolf stood up and went outside. He stood in the shadow beside the swinging door and waited. Soon, he heard somebody walking on the roof above the boardwalk. He followed the sound to the side of the saloon and saw a man jump from the roof to the ground.

"Hello, JB," Little Man Wolf said.

"Who are you? I don't know you. You have been dogging my trail for days. Why?"

Little Man Wolf did not say anything.

"Why don't you say something?"

Little Man Wolf walked out of the shadow, and they stood, facing each other. JB looked at him for a long time.

"You looked taller in the saddle," JB said.

"Does it matter how tall I am?"

JB looked at the bandoleer with the Colts in the holsters. He also noted the Bowie knife and tomahawk hanging on the man's sides.

"If you are a bounty hunter, you have the wrong man."

"I have the right man."

"I'm not wanted in this state."

"You should be."

"Who are you?"

"McCall's the name."

"McCall. Where did I hear that name before?"

"Eight years ago. A farm near Prescott, Arizona."

"Eight years ago?"

"Jesse Fremont says hello."

"Are you trying to be funny? Jesse Fremont is dead."

"Then, maybe you can say hello to him when you see him."

"See him where?"

"Hell, of course."

It suddenly dawned on him that this was the Jeremiah McCall who killed Jesse Fremont and Tom Baxter at Betsy's Saloon in Nogales. Without saying another word JB drew his gun. Before he could even cock it, a Bowie knife hit him in the chest, piercing his heart.

Little Man Wolf walked over slowly, and looked at the man as he lay on the ground with eyes still wide open in disbelief. He twisted the knife left and right before pulling it out. Then, he wiped it clean on the man's shirt.

"Let's go," he said to Lhachaeh. "We still have a long way to go."

CHAPTER XIX

From a distance Little Man Wolf could hear the whistle of the Atchison, Topeka,& Santa Fe train warning horses and riders to get off its tracks as it prepared to leave the station. He could see hundreds of people walking about on the street, and riders going in and out of the town. Wagon teams hauling piles of animal bones made their way to Dodge City.

"What are those?" Little Man Wolf asked one of the teamsters.

"Buffalo bones," the man replied. A skinny ten-year-old boy sat next to him. He wore an old crumpled shirt that seemed to have been darned more than a hundred times.

"Where'd you get them?"

"Gathered them up out in the range. Don't belong to no one, except them dead carcasses. Hunters don't want 'em. They just want the hide."

"What will you do with them?"

"Sell them in town. Maybe get a new shirt for my boy here and something nice for my woman's hair. The rest go for food supplies. Crop has been bad for a spell, what with this drought."

"I'm sorry about that."

"Yep, this drought will go on for a while. Been bad. Really bad. These buffalo bones are the only ones feeding my family."

"What will the buyers do with those bones?"

"Send them east. I heard they ship them to England where they

grind them, and mix them with clay to make them fancy porcelain dishes."

The teamster turned to have a better look at the man he was talking to. He noticed the bandoleer with the two six-shooters.

"Mister, those guns of yours—you have to check those in at Wright & Beverly when you go into town," he said to Little Man Wolf.

"Why?"

"City ordinance. You can't have guns if you're going to the north side of the tracks. Charlie Basset, the Marshall, is very particular about that. He'll throw you in jail, or you'll end up in Boot Hill cemetery. South side is okay with those guns, but that's a rough neighborhood."

"Thanks for letting me know."

"You're welcome. Best to keep out of trouble in this town. They have the toughest group of lawmen here. The toughest are Bat Masterson and Wyatt Earp."

"Wyatt Earp is here?"

"He is one of the deputy marshals. You know him?"

"A long time ago. I was a still a little boy. Well, good day sir, I'll see you around."

"Best to keep out of trouble, young man."

The strong odor of buffalo hide assailed his senses as he entered Dodge City. Thousands of Buffalo hides were piled higher than one story. They were right on the street beside the railroad track waiting for the next train with more cargo cars.

"This may be the last shipment," said a buffalo man talking to the railroad agent. "There are no more buffalo out there."

"How much have you got there?" the railroad agent asked.

"About forty thousand hides."

A group of cowboys were guiding a herd of Texas longhorns into town. There must have been at least ten thousand heads in that bunch.

"There's your next source of business," the buffalo man said to the railroad agent, pointing to the herd of Texas cattle.

The railroad man turned to look. "They drive in every week now," he said. "The buyers and sellers meet here in Dodge City, even the quartermasters from the forts. There's a big drive coming in next week—Seventy-five thousand heads. They're on the Chisholm Trail now. Over a hundred cowboys are bringing them in. There will be a real wild night on the south side when that bunch comes in."

Little Man Wolf went directly to one of the saloons on the south side. There were hundreds of them all over town. The one he went to was quiet, with only two customers sipping their beer at each end of the bar. There were no women around. An old oriental man was sweeping the floor. The bartender was facing the wall and did not see Little Man Wolf when he came in and sat at a table. He turned around and came out from behind the bar.

"Would you like to come over and drink at the bar? It's early, and everybody's still asleep. I have to do every thing," the bartender said.

"I can't drink at the bar. It's too high for me, and I don't want to stand on a chair."

Little Man Wolf extended his legs from under the table for the bartender to see. The bartender looked at the legs, and then at Little Man Wolf.

"I'm sorry, I didn't know," the bartender said.

"No apology needed."

"What will you have?"

"Cold beer?"

"You got it."

"Also, do you have anything for my friend here? He's hungry. I'll pay extra for it," Little Man Wolf said as he patted Lhachaeh's head.

"No need to. I'll get something."

The bartender left and came back right away with the beer and plate for Lhachaeh.

"The first one is on me," he said.

"Thanks," Little Man Wolf replied with a smile.

Little Man Wolf noticed the oriental man after the bartender went

back to his place. There was something familiar with this man.

"*Ni hao ma*," Little Man Wolf said.

The oriental man stopped and looked up from what he was doing.

"Do I know you?" the oriental man asked.

"My name is Abe Lincoln," Little Man Wolf said.

"Abe Lincoln?"

There was a long hesitation.

"Played a little trick on you, *Shifu*."

"Jeremiah!" the oriental man suddenly blurted out.

"It's Little Man Wolf, *Shifu*. No more Jeremiah. *Pequeno Hombre Lobo*."

"Call me Lee Bok. I don't have students here."

"How are you Lee Bok? You're are a long way from the mines in Arizona."

"The mine closed down and everybody scattered. You are all grown-up now. I heard about your parents. So sorry."

"My uncle, Wrestling Bear took me to my grandparents at Fort Defiance. I grew up among the Navajo—my mother's tribe."

"What you doing here in Dodge City?"

"I'm looking for a man named Anderson. Wild Tommy Anderson, they call him."

"Is he a buffalo hunter?"

"No. Works mostly as a cowboy, if he's not robbing somebody."

"Cowboys come and go in this town. Let you know if I hear something. Where will you be?"

"I don't know yet, but I know where to find you. I'll come around."

"Who was that man, Lee Bok?" the bartender later asked.

"My friend Little Man Wolf."

"That's what I thought."

Little Man Wolf was not inclined to check in his guns at Wright & Beverly as required by the city ordinance, so he stayed on the south side of the town. Besides, Wild Tommy Anderson, if in town, would most likely be on the south side himself where there were saloons, dance halls, and brothels on every street. The hotel rooms were small, and not well kept considering the high price the owners were charging for them. But, everything was expensive in Dodge City. It was the price one had to pay for the town's prosperity.

He boarded Running Wind in a stable with instructions to keep it well fed and brushed down daily. Running Wind did not seem happy being boarded and pampered. It would rather be out in the open with his two companions. Lhachaeh was easier to take around, although there were places that would not allow dogs at all.

That night the cowboys who brought in the ten thousand heads of Texas Longhorns were shooting up the town. They got paid that afternoon, and were boozing it up, gambling and grabbing all the women they could get. A fight broke out between them and another group in the saloon. The fight got bigger and bigger, and somebody called the marshal.

Wyatt Earp rushed in from outside right into the middle of the brawl and started hitting the rowdies in the head with the butt of his gun.

Little Man Wolf was sitting at a small table by the wall beside a bigger table where four men were playing poker. From where he sat, he had a good view of the whole floor and the happenings. During the fight, a cowboy sitting with a group at the opposite side of the room drew his gun slowly and took aim at Wyatt Earp. Little Man Wolf drew his gun, and was about to shoot the cowboy when somebody at the table next to him yelled, "Look out Wyatt!"

Wyatt spun around with the cowboy he was holding, and using him as a shield, pointed his gun at the man at the table who was about to shoot him. The man was surprised to see three guns pointed at him. He quickly holstered his gun, and raised his hands in the air.

The man who yelled to warn Wyatt looked at Little Man Wolf and asked, "Were you going to shoot the cowboy, too."

"I guess I didn't have to since you had your gun out already."

The other deputies came and took away the rowdies, including

the man who was about to shoot Wyatt.

"Thanks, Doc," Wyatt Earp said when he came over. "I didn't know you were sitting there."

"Thank this man, too. He actually drew faster than I did."

"Thank you. Do I know you? You are new around here."

Little Man Wolf stood up. Wyatt Earp looked at him and had instant recognition.

"Either One!" Wyatt Earp exclaimed.

"It's just Little Man Wolf now, Wyatt. There's no more Jeremiah. So, there's no more Either One."

Wyatt Earp smiled remembering how he used to tease Little Man Wolf.

"Doc, this is Little Man Wolf. I knew his family back in Arizona. Little Man Wolf, this is my friend Doc Holliday."

"You're the famous Doc Holliday," Little Man Wolf said. "I'm pleased to meet you, sir."

"I'm a dentist. I pull teeth. I guess some of my unhappy patients have talked about me. You are a polite young man. I can see you are well schooled."

"I was a student of Padre Tomas of Fort Defiance, sir."

"Preacher? I know Preacher. He not only teaches about the good book, but also about other things. Now it makes sense to me. The bandoleer, the two guns and the lightning draw. You had a good teacher. There is none better than Preacher," Doc Holliday said. "I love that old man. He is a good friend."

"What brings you here Little Man Wolf?" Wyatt asked.

"I'm looking for a man named Wild Tommy Anderson."

"I heard about your folks. I'm sorry. I know about the incident at Betsy's Saloon in Nogales, and the one in Laguna. It didn't occur to me that it was you. You were still a boy the last time I saw you."

"Am I wanted?"

"Don't worry, you're in the clear. The authorities just need to keep track of everybody. But, you're building quite a reputation already. Just don't make any mistake and cross the line. I'd hate to take you in."

"Thanks, Wyatt."

"Listen. There's a performance tomorrow night at the Comique Variety Hall. A comedian named Eddie Foy is in town. Why don't you come? Doc Holliday will be there too."

"Thanks. I have never been in a theatre before. I'd love to see a performance."

"Good. I'll walk out with you. Doc, sorry to disrupt your poker game."

"Just don't do it again, Wyatt," Doc Holliday said as he sat down to play cards.

"Doc. It was nice meeting you. I'll see you tonight at the theatre."

"Likewise, Little Man Wolf. See you."

Outside, Lhachaeh immediately got up when Little Man Wolf came out. Wyatt Earp looked at the dog and said, "Is this the dog I gave you?"

Lhachaeh was already wagging its tail.

"Look," Little Man Wolf said. "He remembers you."

"It can't be. It was barely two months old when I gave it to you."

"Lhachaeh is a very smart dog. You won't believe what he is capable of doing."

Wyatt Earp got down on his knees and played with the dog.

"You did give it a good home."

CHAPTER XX

Wyatt Earp was standing outside the Comique Variety Hall with another man when Little Man Wolf arrived. The night was still early and the performers were preparing for their show.

"I'm glad you could make it," Wyatt said.

"I wouldn't miss it for anything."

"James, this is my friend Little Man Wolf. This is Deputy Marshal James Masterson."

"Pleased to meet you sir."

"Likewise."

"You brought Lhachaeh," Wyatt Earp said, patting the dog's head.

Lhachaeh was wagging its tail.

"He's with me all the time," Little Man Wolf said. "Where is Doc Holliday? I thought he was coming too."

"Here's already inside with Ford County Marshal Bat Masterson, James's brother. It was too hot in there. I thought I'd stay out here until they're ready."

"Pardon me for staring, Little Man Wolf. You're the man Doc Holliday was telling us about earlier," James Masterson said. "You're much younger than I thought."

"I'll be seventeen soon."

"And, you're already getting quite a reputation."

"Yes, we already know all about it," Wyatt Earp interceded.

"The Mexicans were talking when you rode in. They recognized you. They said you killed eighteen bandits all by yourself," James Masterson said.

"I didn't know about this," Wyatt Earp said.

"The Mexicans call him *Navajo Blanco*. He killed eighteen bandits when he was only fourteen."

"Is it true?" Wyatt asked.

"No," Little Man Wolf said. "Fifteen. I killed only fifteen."

"Son of a gun," Wyatt said incredulously.

"So far as I can see and have heard, you're a good man Little Man Wolf. Just be careful you don't cross the line. One little mistake, and you're on the other side of the law," James Masterson said.

"He knows. I already told him that," Wyatt said.

Just as Wyatt finished his sentence, a man galloped by on horseback and unloaded his six-guns at the three men. Instinctively, Little Man Wolf crouched, drew his guns, turned and returned fire at the fleeing rider. Two other shots rang out as Wyatt and James also returned fire. The man fell off his horse. The three men ran over to the fallen shooter.

"George Hoyt!" Wyatt said.

"We should have put him on his horse and kicked him out of town last night when he was shooting up the streets," James Masterson said.

Doc Holliday and Bat Masterson came running with their guns drawn.

"Who is it?" Bat Masterson asked.

"George Hoyt, the cowboy who was creating a lot of ruckus last night," James said.

"Is he dead?" Doc Holliday asked.

"No, but he is badly wounded," Wyatt said.

"Who got him?" Doc asked.

"I don't rightly know. We all returned fire," Wyatt said. "Maybe Little Man Wolf did. He was the first to fire back."

They all looked at Little Man Wolf.

"I know who you are," Bat Masterson said. "Doc already told us. There will be an inquiry. It's best for everybody to say one of the marshals shot him."

Little Man Wolf spent most of his time that summer watching all the cattle drives come into Dodge City. Some of the cowboys he spoke to knew Wild Tommy Anderson. They even worked with him on some cattle drives. He might be in the next cattle drive coming from Texas, some would say. Little Man Wolf also checked the saloons every night in case Wild Tommy Anderson was not in any cattle drive, but had ridden into town on his own. He also spoke with Lee Bok several times to see if his network of Chinese workers had any information. Little Man Wolf knew that Dodge City was the favorite stop of Wild Tommy Anderson, and was bound to show up any day. It was just a matter of being patient.

One night early that fall, the hotel manager woke Little Man Wolf up.

"Deputy Marshal Wyatt Earp is downstairs looking for you. He wants you to get dressed and come down right away. I think something really bad has happened," the hotel manager said.

Little Man Wolf and Lhachaeh came down shortly. Wyatt Earp was pacing impatiently.

"I'm sorry to get you out of bed this early, but I need your help," Wyatt Earp said. "Dora Hand, the opera singer, who was a houseguest of Mayor James Kelly was shot dead around four-o-clock this morning. Mayor Kelly and his wife are away for a few days, and Miss Hand was sleeping in their bed. We think whoever shot her intended to shoot Mayor Kelly. A few days ago, the son of a rich cattleman, James Kennedy, had an altercation with Mayor Kelly. Everyone thought the affair was settled when Kennedy left for Kansas City. But, very early this morning, some witnesses claimed they saw Kennedy in town riding in the direction of Mayor Kelly's house."

"How can I help?" Little Man Wolf asked.

"We are organizing a posse, and may take a few a hours to get everybody together. In the meantime, we need a tracker who will go ahead and leave us signs to follow."

"I'll get Running Wind from the stable."

"I'll meet you at the Mayor's house. Marshal Charlie Bassett is up there now."

At the Mayor's house, Marshal Charlie Bassett met Little Man Wolf.

"No need for introductions. I know who you are. Thank you for agreeing to help, Little Man Wolf. Let me deputize you to make it official"

After the swearing in, Marshal Charlie Bassett gave Little Man Wolf a briefing. He showed him the possible position of the shooter from the ground, the trajectory from the bedroom side, and the position of the victim. Then they went down and inspected the grounds and the tracks left by the horse. Lhachaeh sniffed around.

"He probably rode back to Kansas City," Marshall Bassett said.

"Kansas City is east. The tracks say he went south," Little Man Wolf said. "No, he wasn't going to Kansas City. He is headed in the direction of Oklahoma. I will ride ahead and leave you signs to follow."

"What kind of signs?"

"You'll know when you see them."

He was off on Running Wind, with Lhachaeh alongside.

Little Man Wolf followed the tracks the whole day. Toward evening, the tracks went southwest. Little Man Wolf decided to camp and wait for the posse to catch up. At dawn, the posse came. They had been riding all night.

"Those were some signs you left for us. You couldn't miss them even in the dark," Wyatt Earp said.

"I knew you would be riding all night. I thought I'd make it easier for you."

"You know all these gentlemen, Little Man Wolf. Wyatt, Bat Masterson, Bill Tilghman, and William Duffy," Marshal Bassett said. "What do you have?"

"He is riding toward Mead City. We can cut across now, and head him off. He won't be starting off again 'til morning because he thinks nobody is following him."

"Let's ride then."

They set a trap on the road to Mead City. In the morning, they sighted James Kennedy trotting leisurely toward the city. When he was near enough to be unable avoid them, Marshal Bassett stood up, fired a warning shot and ordered Kennedy to surrender. Kennedy whirled around and kicked his horse to a gallop. Shots were fired hitting Kennedy in the shoulder. Four other shots hit the horse, killing it instantly. It fell on top of Kennedy. Bat Masterson ran over and yanked James Kennedy from under his horse.

"I'll get even with you!" James Kennedy kept screaming at Bat Masterson as he was being pulled out.

Later that month the last batch of cattle from Texas was driven into town—twenty-five thousand head of cattle in all. Winter would blow in soon, during which time all cattle drives were halted until spring. Little Man Wolf felt that he had been in Dodge City too long, and was getting restless. However, it was too late in the year to move on.

"You have done good work here, why don't you stay on as deputy marshal." Wyatt Earp suggested. "I'll talk to Charlie. I'm sure Marshal Bassett will agree. He likes you. He likes the work you did on the Dora Hand case."

Little Man Wolf did not say anything for a while.

"I never thought of being a lawman," he said, thoughtfully.

"You're a natural for it. You have the right attitude, a sense of fairness, and strength of character. You're handy with the gun, and you're not afraid of anything."

"I still have my work to do. It's not finished."

"I know that. But, there's nothing you can do about that right now. You spend a lot of time going from one saloon to another every night looking for your man. You might as well do it behind a badge and get paid for it."

Two nights later, Little Man Wolf was checking the bars and dance halls with a shiny badge on his chest. He did not move his residence to the north side of the tracks, although he could now walk around there freely with his guns. He had already a made a lot of friends on the south side, and it made more sense to be where the man he's looking for would mostly likely be.

Except for a couple of brawls and non-fatal shootings that Little Man Wolf had to pacify and mediate, the season passed quickly and uneventfully. He spent most of his free time with Lee Bok, practicing his *wushu* techniques. Lee Bok had started a secret martial arts school in the Chinese district of the town. None of the town deputies bothered to go there, except for Little Man Wolf. This left them quite free to practice.

Early in the summer, the cattle drives started coming in every day. At two o'clock past midnight, after a drive came in, Lee Bok met Little Man Wolf on the street as he walked the beat with Lhachaeh. Lee Bok had been looking for him.

"The man you look for," Lee Bok began. "He is at Blue Star Saloon with five cowboys. Be careful."

As he always did, Little Man Wolf looked in from the outside window to assess the situation. He slowly opened the swinging door and walked in. The dog was a familiar sight by now in Dodge City, and nobody took a second look. The din in the saloon became louder when they walked in.

"Look, they're hiring little boys now as deputy marshal. Is that badge real, kid?" one of cowboys said. The group laughed.

"That's not a boy, that's a little man," another cowboy said, and their laughter became louder. "Hey Tommy—look—a little man playing deputy."

"Careful boys, that's Deputy Marshal Little Man Wolf," Sam, the bartender warned the cowboys, as he wiped the counter.

"Little Man Wolf," Wild Tommy Anderson said. "Where did I hear that name before?"

"Are you Wild Tommy Anderson?" Little Man Wolf asked.

"What of it?"

"I'm bringing you in for the murder of Victor McCall and his wife Laughing Deer in Arizona nine years ago."

The cowboys laughed again.

"You must be out of your mind. Nine years ago? Nobody cares about a squaw man and his bitch around here."

"The law is the same anywhere."

"Now, I know who you are. You're the one who killed Jesse Fremont and Tom Baxter in Nogales and JB in Laguna. You've been asking about me since last year. You're no lawman. You're a bounty hunter."

"Hey, little man, why don't you just go away," one of the cowboys said. "Nobody is taking away our friend here."

"Don't get involved if you're clean," Little Man Wolf said.

"Well, clean or not, there are five of us, and we stand with Wild Tommy here. You're just a little man what can you do?"

Wild Tommy Anderson by now realized who Little Man Wolf was, and his reputation with the gun. He was not going to take any chances. He turned his back to face the bar, and drank his liquor from the glass. On Tommy's signal, all six men turned to face Little Man Wolf, drawing and cocking their guns, ready to shoot.

Little Man Wolf anticipated their plan, and he moved two steps to the right as the men turned their backs. In a split second, six cowboys lay dead on the floor. Wild Tommy and one other cowboy were able to get out one shot each, but they had shot in the wrong direction.

Within a few minutes, Wyatt Earp and Bat Masterson barged in with guns drawn. They saw the dead cowboys on the floor.

"What happened?" Wyatt asked.

"The deputy tried to arrest that man called Wild Tommy Anderson, and the five cowboys with him turned on the deputy," a voice in the back of the room said.

"Who said that?"

"It's me Doc Holliday."

"Who drew first?" Bat Masterson asked.

"The cowboys did."

"That's true, Sheriff," Sam, the bartender, said. "I told them that's Deputy Marshall Little Man Wolf. They didn't listen."

"Anyone else who saw what happened?" Bat Masterson asked.

Five other men backed-up Sam's story.

"Fine. Somebody get the coroner and get these bodies out of here," Bat Masterson said.

Outside, Wyatt Earp, Bat Masterson and Doc Holliday conferred with Little Man Wolf.

"Doc, I didn't see you in there. Would you have helped?" Little Man Wolf asked.

"If I thought you needed help. But, you didn't," Doc Holliday said.

"I'll pay for their funeral," Little Man Wolf volunteered.

"No need to," Wyatt said. "The city will take care of it. It won't cost them much anyway."

The following morning, the bodies were buried on Boot Hill in a common grave with no coffins. A marker was set up with following inscription:

"Here lie Wild Tommy Anderson,
and five of his friends
who stood with him against
Deputy Marshal Little Man Wolf.
Now, all friends stand (or lie) together in hell."

Around November of that year, Wyatt Earp told Little Man Wolf that he was leaving for Tombstone, Arizona with his older brothers James and Virgil. Doc Holliday left for Trinidad, Colorado late in the summer in search of a good game of poker.

"Why don't you come with us?"

"What will you be doing out there?" Little Man Wolf asked.

"Virgil has been offered the position of Deputy U.S. Marshal in the southwest territory. James and I will stake a claim for silver mining. The town is booming from silver mining. You can be a partner with us."

"That's very generous of you, Wyatt. But I have to finish my duty to my family. I will look you up when it's done."

"What's your plan now?"

"I'll stay until spring and then I'll go south to Texas. I'm looking for a man named Cherokee Lee. Word is, he is holed up in El Paso."

"Good Luck, then."

"You too, Wyatt. I hope your venture succeeds."

CHAPTER XXI

Little Man Wolf did not leave Dodge City as he planned at the onset of the spring of '80. Wyatt left in December, leaving the city short of officers while the cattle drives started to come in. Marshal Charlie Bassett prevailed upon Little Man Wolf to stay until qualified replacements were hired.

The nights in Dodge City were the same as any other nights when cattle drives came in. Cowboys got paid, got drunk, got into fights over women, and shot up the places and the streets. Little Man Wolf rarely had to draw his guns to control the ruckus. He would simply walk over to the rowdiest man, sweep him off his feet with techniques he learned from Lee Bok, and hit him over the head with the dull end of his tomahawk. Occasionally, a greater force would be required to bring down a big, strong man. In these times, he would kick the inside of the knee at the joint. Sometimes the knee got broken, but Little Man Wolf preferred that over having to shoot the man. Lhachaeh was always there to control the other men. Then he would get the other men in the group to pick up their friend and bring him over to jail to sleep it off.

When it was finally time to leave in August, he went over to the Chinese section and said goodbye to Lee Bok and all his friends. He thanked Marshal Charlie Basset and the Masterson brothers.

"I'm planning to leave around November this year. I will turn the office over to Jim Masterson," Marshal Charlie Bassett said.

"What will you do?" Little Man Wolf asked.

"I don't know yet. I just have to move on."

Little Man Wolf would take the southwest trail until he reached Rio Grande, then follow it down to El Paso. Running Wind was visibly excited about being out in the open again, and galloping for a longer period. It had gained weight with long stretches of inactivity, being overfed, and pampered with brush downs. Lhachaeh was happy too that they were on the move again. It was keeping pace with Running Wind, but it was obvious that age was beginning to slow it down.

They had been traveling for a week without meeting anyone. Little Man Wolf had avoided going to towns because it would mean delays, distractions and perhaps unexpected trouble that could divert him from his mission.

On the morning of the tenth day, they ran into two companies of U.S. Cavalry. The soldiers were all black men, including the captain.

"Good morning, sir. I'm Captain Louis Carpenter of the 10th U.S. Cavalry."

"Good morning."

"May I ask your name?"

"Little Man Wolf."

The captain looked at him closer.

"Also known as Jeremiah McCall."

"Where does the name Little Man Wolf come from, Mr. McCall?"

"My mother was a Navajo."

"I see. What, may I ask, are you doing out here on the range by yourself?"

"I just rode in from Kansas on my way to El Paso. Is there any problem I should know about?"

"We have been in pursuit of hostile Apache the whole night. They raided places in Socorro, and have been seen in this area. Their leader, Victorio, is a vicious man. He tortures his captives before killing them."

"I have not seen any Apache. In fact, I have not seen a single soul since I left Kansas."

"Victorio can appear from out of nowhere, do his killing, and disappear just as quickly. I would keep my eyes open, Mr. McCall. In fact, I suggest you ride with us."

"Thank you for your concern, Captain. I will be fine."

"Just watch yourself. Don't take any chances."

"I won't."

Little Man Wolf remembered Chief Victorio, the Mescalero Apache leader at the Bosque Redondo reservation, when he was there briefly as a little boy. This was before his father came with Colonel Kit Carson, and had him released with his mother from the reservation. Chief Victorio spent most of his time talking to his grandfather, Red Lance. They knew each other. The chief seemed to be a kind man. He even heard him laugh once.

He followed the Rio Grande as he rode south. His mind was still on Chief Victorio. He wondered what made a kind man change into a brutal predator, if what Captain Carpenter said was true.

Suddenly, an Apache brave jumped him from a boulder. He heard Lhachaeh bark a warning, but it happened so fast he had no time to react. They both tumbled off Running Wind. The Apache had a knife and started slashing. Little Man Wolf had the chance to pull out his gun and shoot, but he did not want to kill the warrior. Instead, he yelled out in the Apache language that he did not want to fight. The warrior kept slashing. Little Man Wolf did not even pull out his Bowie knife. He evaded and he blocked the knife hand, and with a quick movement, disarmed the warrior. When he turned, there were at least twenty Apache warriors surrounding him.

"You fight well, white man," a man on a white horse said.

Little Man Wolf recognized him right away as Chief Victorio.

"You had your guns and your knife, why didn't you pull them out."

"I did not want to kill him."

"Why not, he would have killed you?"

"I have no quarrel with the Apache. I yelled to him that I did not want to fight—that I am a friend, not an enemy. But he would not stop."

"I heard you. But, he cannot hear you. He is deaf."

"I'm sorry."

"That is a Navajo horse you are riding, and you speak the Apache tongue well. Where did you learn?"

"I was born to Laughing Deer of the Diné Towering House People clan, and born for Victor McCall of the Irish People."

"You learned well. I remember a little Navajo boy with golden hair who belonged to the clan of my friend Red Lance."

"Red Lance is my grandfather."

"What is your name?"

"Little Man Wolf."

"I have heard of you. The Mexicans also call you *Navajo Blanco*. You are the great warrior who rode with the Diné Chief Manuelito."

"That was a long time ago."

"This is my sister Lozen. She is my bravest warrior," Chief Victorio nodded in the direction of a woman beside him on a magnificent looking horse. "She has killed hundreds of Mexican soldiers and scalp hunters, too."

Little Man Wolf acknowledged the introduction in the Apache way.

"Chief Victorio, there are two companies of soldiers ten miles back looking for you. They know you are here."

"Buffalo soldiers?"

"U.S. Cavalry."

"Yes, black men soldiers. Good fighters. Better than white soldiers."

"They could be around here right now."

"No. We know where they are. They go to Rattlesnake Spring in Texas. They wait for us but they won't find us. We vanish in the wind. Where do you go now?" Chief Victorio asked.

"El Paso."

"You may go in peace Little Man Wolf."

He reached El Paso two weeks later. There were hundreds of black U.S. Cavalry soldiers gathered in town. The 10th U.S. Cavalry under Colonel Benjamin Grierson, a white man, was bivouacked near the river at the north side of town. People were talking about a big battle at Rattlesnake Spring with the Apache band of Chief Victorio.

As Little Man Wolf rode into town, a cavalry captain met him.

"I'm glad you made it safely, Mr. McCall," the captain said.

"Captain Carpenter, isn't it?"

"Yes, it's me, Mr. McCall."

"What is going on?"

"We fought Chief Victorio and his band at Rattlesnake Spring, but they escaped back to Mexico. Colonel Grierson is waiting for clearance to cross the Rio Grande and continue pursuit into Mexico. The Mexican army is hunting them on the other side. We have him boxed in. We might see the end of this campaign soon."

Little Man Wolf went directly to a saloon. The saloons were always the best places to find out what went on in a town. By that evening, Little Man Wolf had learned that a well-known town citizen named John Hale owned a ranch about 13 miles northwest of El Paso in the Upper Valley. This man was reputed to be a cattle rustler, and he had powerful friends who protected him. Friends like former town Marshal George Campbell, Deputy Marshal Bill Johnson, and the Manning brothers: Doc Manning, James Manning and Frank Manning. They were all considered community leaders and upright citizens of El Paso. John Hale had three known gunmen working for him who would rustle and kill for him. They were named Cherokee Lee, Pervey, and Fredericks.

Little Man Wolf did not know Pervey and Fredericks and had no interest in them. Cherokee Lee was the one he was looking for. He went to a gun store, bought two boxes of .44-40 cartridges and asked for directions to the John Hale's ranch.

"Looking for work, are you?" the storeowner asked.

"Maybe."

"Are you handy with those fancy Colts you're carrying?"

"Pretty much."

"Hale will hire you on the spot if you can show how handy you are with those shooting irons."

"We'll see. Thanks for the direction."

"You bet."

Little Man Wolf spent several days observing (from a distance) the activity at the Hale ranch. Everyday, the three rustlers brought in cattle from somewhere. Then they spent the rest of the day branding those cattle. In the evening they rode into town and spent the rest of the night drinking or whoring. Little Man Wolf considered the opportunity in accomplishing his mission. The possibility of confronting Cherokee Lee in town was out of the question. Witnesses would most likely be against him.

He could stop him on the trail, but then he always rode with Pervey and Fredericks. It would be unnecessary killing if he had to take on all three. He just wanted Cherokee Lee.

Little Man Wolf always made sure that Cherokee Lee never had a full view of him when he was in town, lest he notice his physical stature and make a connection. By now, the story about Jesse Fremont and Tom Baxter and the others was widespread. One night Little Man Wolf was sitting close enough to hear the conversation between Cherokee Lee and his two friends.

"Are you going to see your lady in Juarez tonight?" the man called Pervey asked.

"Not tonight. Saturday. She loves to go to church on Sundays after I see her—to confess her sins," Cherokee Lee said, and they all laugh.

"What if the husband is there?" Fredericks asked.

"I take her anyway."

"Husband says nothing?"

"What can he say? I'll shoot him if opens his mouth."

"That's the cantina just across the river, isn't it?"

"Yes, Carmen's Cantina. The husband named it after her."

"I've been there. I've seen your woman. She is beautiful. I would kill you for her if I were the husband," Pervey said.

Cherokee Lee pulled out a gun and put it on the table.

"I'm just joking," Pervey said.

Little Man Wolf went to Carmen's Cantina across the Rio Grande every night of that week. He checked out the entire vicinity around the place. He made friends with the people in there, and made sure that after a few days, his presence would not be considered unusual. Contrary to his expectation the place was not a dance hall but a restaurant, and Carmen, wife of the owner, was not a whore. He ate supper there every night, and drank the local beer. He was always generous with the tip.

On Friday morning, he woke up to the news that Chief Victorio was ambushed and killed by the Mexican army at Tres Castillos Mountains, Chihuahua—about seventy miles south of El Paso—that morning of October 15, 1880. Little Man Wolf lay in bed for a long time. The vivid memory of Canyon de Chelly and the hard march to Bosque Redondo was revived in his mind. Did Chief Victorio and his people not have the right to live? he asked himself. He thought of Lozen. Did they kill her too? Then the image of his father and mother came to mind. It had been ten years and they still could not complete their journey to the next world. He had to finish his mission, and let the spirits of his parents rest in peace.

That evening at the cantina, Little Man Wolf overheard the husband and wife talking about Cherokee Lee. It seemed that his presence was not really welcome, and Carmen was afraid for her husband's life if he did something as foolish as trying to shoot Cherokee Lee.

"He is a *pistolero*. You would not have a chance at all, Pedro," she said.

"This is killing me. I must do something."

"We can just pray."

On Saturday night, Little Man Wolf came earlier than usual and selected the table with the best view of the whole place. It would be a long night, he expected. Cherokee Lee would not come until he was completely boozed up.

At around eleven in the evening, all the diners had left for home. A few men were left drinking tequila. The door to the cantina swung open, and bounced back against the wall. Lhachaeh got up immediately from the floor, keeping its head down while eyeing the newcomer.

"Where's Carmen, *mi amor*? There you are. Come here," Cherokee Lee commanded.

Cherokee Lee forced Carmen to sit on his lap, and started kissing her neck and touching her breast.

"Let's go upstairs to your room."

"No. *No mas*."

"What do you mean no. I said let's go."

"No. No more."

Cherokee Lee slapped her hard across the face. He drew his gun, and aimed it at Pedro.

"I'll shoot your husband if you don't come."

"Please, don't. Please don't."

Cherokee Lee started dragging her toward the stairs.

Little Man Wolf stood up.

"Cherokee Lee," he said in a deep, strong voice.

"Who called?"

"Let her go."

Cherokee Lee was surprised to hear somebody speak.

"Who the hell are you?" he asked, shoving Carmen aside.

"The name is Jeremiah McCall."

"I don't know you. Why don't you mind your own business before you get hurt?"

"The McCall farm near Prescott, Arizona, ten years ago."

"Oh, yeah the squaw man. I still remember his wife. She had the most beautiful body I've seen. You're the kid? We thought you died in the fire."

"Not quite."

"You didn't grow much did you? The fire stunted your growth?"

Little Man Wolf did not say anything.

"What do you want to do little man, beat me up?"

"I can do that, or I can just kill you."

"Or you can what? Don't you see the gun in my hand?"

"I see it."

"Do you think you are fast enough to beat me when I already have the gun in my hand?"

"Yes."

"You idiot!" Cherokee Lee yelled as he raised his gun to point at Little Man Wolf.

He was able to raise his gun halfway before four bullets hit him in the chest and throat, throwing him over the table to the wall. Cherokee Lee made a gurgling sound as blood rushed to his windpipe, choking him. Then he lay still.

For almost a full minute, nobody in the room could say anything. They had never seen anything like it before. The lightning speed with which Little Man Wolf drew his two guns, shot the man before he could even blink, and then holster the guns again with a quick twirl and turn amazed them.

"*Dios mio. Dios mio,*" Carmen kept repeating as she picked herself up from the floor.

Pedro was the first one to speak.

"*Señor Lobo*. You have killed the man."

"I know."

"I don't know how to thank you," Pedro said. "You have answered my prayers."

"You must go quickly," Carmen said. "Do not go back to El Paso. When the Mexican authorities come we will tell them he had a fight with a big, bad gringo who shot him and rode back to El Paso. If his American friends come, we will tell them Mexican *bandidos* killed him. Go now, please. And *Señor Lobo, muchas gracias*."

"*De nada*."

CHAPTER XXII

The darkened sky suddenly opened up and torrential rain came down. A flash of lightning hit a tree about a hundred feet away, shearing off its top. Running Wind reacted briefly to the deafening sound of thunder, but quickly recovered.

"We have to make it across the river before the water swells, boys." He was talking to Lhachaeh and Running Wind.

Cautiously, Little Man Wolf directed Running Wind to the shallow part of the river. Lhachaeh started to swim across. Just as they reached the embankment on the other side of the river there was a loud explosion. A huge flood of water came rushing down from upstream carrying with it fallen trees.

Little Man Wolf could see some flickering lights at a distance. That would be the Mexican town, he thought.

They made their way through the muddy path and reached the town just as another lightning flashed against the sky. The rain started to abate.

Little Man Wolf followed the sound of guitar playing and the unmistakable sound of castanets to a dimly lit cantina. He jumped off Running Wind, looped the rein loosely at the bar by the trough, and said, "We may not be staying here long boys."

He looked in through the glass window and saw a man sitting on a stool playing the guitar, and a dark haired woman dancing the flamenco. There were four men in a corner playing cards. He thought he recognized a gringo with a funny looking hat with a green band. It was Billy the Kid. It had been three years since he met him on the range in New Mexico. Another gringo sat across the table from Billy. That could be the heavyset man he was trailing. He was the only other gringo in the place. There were at least twenty Mexican men and some women inside, drinking and laughing. The men were all heavily armed with six-shooters and rifles.

As soon as Little Man Wolf entered the cantina, the music stopped. Everybody looked at him. Lhachaeh stayed outside by the door looking in. The dog was agitated, but it stayed lying on the boardwalk. Little Man Wolf looked around. Billy the Kid was looking at him, but did not show a sign of recognition.

"Give me another card," Billy said to the other gringo who was dealing.

The gringo gave him another card, but he kept looking at Little Man Wolf.

"A table *hefe*?"

"Yes, *por favor*, and bring me a bottle of tequila and a glass."

"*Si, señor*, right away."

"Wait. Do you have any food?"

"We have enchiladas, rice, and beans."

"Good. Bring me two plates of that."

"Two plates, *señor*?"

"Yes."

When the man returned Little Man Wolf said, "Take this plate to my friend over there."

"What friend, *señor*?"

"The *perro* by the door."

"Oh yes, of course."

"Can you get a bag of oats for my horse?"

"*Si*, I can send the *niño* to the stable."

"Thank you. Here." Little Man Wolf handed him two silver dollars.

"This takes care of everything, *gracias señor*."

"*De nada.*"

The guitar music started again, and the dark haired woman began clicking the castanets and tapping her shoes.

After he finished eating, a fat man came over.

"You want a woman *señor*?"

"Maybe later," Little Man Wolf said, smiling.

"Do you want her?" the man said, pointing with his lips at the woman dancing the flamenco. "She dances even better in bed."

"I will let you know later."

The fat man walked away shaking his head left to right.

"I'm out," the gringo said, standing up from the table, looking at Little Man Wolf from the side of his eyes. He walked to the swinging door and looked outside into the darkness.

Lhachaeh started making a low growling sound outside the door.

The gringo walked back to the bar and ordered a drink. He turned around to look at Little Man Wolf.

The flamenco music was getting louder and louder.

The gringo finished his drink and ordered another one.

"One more, Fred?"

"Make it fast."

He drank it in one swig, and then walked back to the door. He looked out again. Then he turned around and faced Little Man Wolf.

"I know who you are. Why don't you get it over with?" the man said.

The music stopped, and everybody moved to the side.

Little Man Wolf stood up. The Mexicans stood up, too. Lhachaeh crept slowly inside the room.

"Do you think you can kill us all?" the gringo said.

"I only want you, Fred McAvoy. That will be enough."

"That was eleven years ago. I even forgot about it already."

"I have not."

"You fool. You will die here tonight, boy."

"So will you."

From the back of the room, Billy the Kid said in a loud voice, "*Tranquilo, compadres!*" as he cocked a sawed-off shot gun.

"This is the man you call *Navajo Blanco*. His name is *Pequeño Hombre Lobo*, and he is a friend of mine. I will shoot anyone who draws a gun against him."

"I stand with Billy," a Mexican *pistolero* said, standing up to his side.

"*Gracias*, Jose."

"*De nada*, patron."

"This is a personal fight between them," Billy the Kid continued. "The gringo was one of the men who killed his father and raped and killed his mother."

The Mexicans understood the reason after he said that, and they all backed off to the sides.

"You're a sonafabitch, Billy."

"Hey, I don't owe you anything," Billy said. "He is all yours Little Man Wolf."

The gringo made a move to draw. Little Man Wolf got out four shots, throwing the man all the way to the end of the room. The booming sound of his guns filled the room, and lingered for a while. The women, and even some of the men, made the sign of the cross. They had never seen a faster draw.

"Do we understand each other?" Billy asked the Mexicans.

"Si, patron."

"Good. *Hasta luego*."

Little Man Wolf, Billy the Kid, and Jose backed up to the door. Lhachaeh was already outside to watch for any surprises.

The rain had stopped, but the road was now thicker with mud.

They all rode slowly north. Nobody came out of the cantina to follow them. After some distance, Little Man Wolf turned to Billy.

"Thanks, Billy. For a while there, I wasn't sure where you stood."

Billy started laughing.

"You are one *loco hombre*, Little Man Wolf. I saw you at the window, looking in. I knew you didn't stand a chance when you walked in. They were all together. You don't have enough bullets in your guns to kill all of them. I didn't want to tip my hand by acknowledging you. I wanted to see how they were going to play it."

"I didn't know the man was a friend of yours."

"The man was no friend of mine. He was even cheating me on the cards. I would have killed him myself if you didn't."

"Thank you, too," Little Man Wolf said to the Mexican.

"*De nada*, Senor Lobo."

"This is Jose Chaves. He fought with me in the Lincoln County War. I trust him with my life."

"I was one of the Regulators with Billy."

"The Mexicans are afraid of Jose Chavez more than they're afraid of me. He is one tough *pistolero*. Jose, would you like to tell Little Man Wolf what you heard."

"*Si*. The two men you killed at Betsy's Saloon have a friend who fought against us in the Lincoln County War. His name is Curly Bill Brosius. He is a very bad *Hombre*. He has about four hundred men working for him rustling cattle at the Mexican border and bringing them to Charleston, near Tombstone, or to Galeyville. He works with Johnny Ringo and the Clanton gang. Word is out that he is looking for you for killing Jesse Fremont and Tom Baxter. You should stay away from those towns."

"Thank you for the information, Jose."

"Be careful."

"I will. Where are you bound for now, Billy?"

"I'm going back to Fort Sumner."

"Billy, there's a $500 reward on your head."

"I know."

"Sheriff Pat Garrett is looking for you up there."

"I'm not worried about Pat. He is a friend of mine."

"I have one more man to track down. I'll see you later."

"Wait. If you run into Curly Bill Brosius, it will be like running into a hornet's nest. Take this sawed-off shotgun and this box of 12-

gauge shots. I have no need for them where I'm going, but you do."

"Thanks, Billy."

"Just watch out for back shooters."

"You too."

CHAPTER XXIII

Little Man Wolf rode slowly into the town of Lordsburg. The first man who saw him quickly went inside his shop, barred the door and pulled down the window shade. Women quickly got their children off the street. Curious men looked through the windows in the shops.

He went directly to the town saloon. It was still late afternoon and the evening crowd had not come in yet. There were only a few men drinking, and sitting lazily with some sleepy-eyed women.

"I'm looking for Ken Stanton, is he here?" Little Man Wolf asked the bartender who was washing and wiping glasses.

"You're Little Man Wolf."

"Is Stanton here?"

"You just missed him. Went out the back door when he heard you were riding into town. You really put the fear of God into him, friend."

"Any idea where he's going?"

"Where he always goes when things get rough for him here in Lordsburg. He went to Galeyville."

"Thanks."

"Wait."

"Galeyville is where all his friends are."

"I figured."

"Listen. That is where Johnny Ringo and Curly Bill Brosius are."

Little Man Wolf stopped and looked at the bartender.

"I know they're looking for you."

"What's your name?"

"Henry."

"You're a good man, Henry. Perhaps I'll see you again later."

The swinging door opened and in walked the town sheriff and two deputies, with guns drawn.

"Put your hands up!"

The bartender turned to look the other way as he kept wiping the glasses.

"What's going on, Sheriff?"

"Little Man Wolf, you were reported seen riding with Billy the Kid and a Mexican bandit named Jose Chaves."

"Yes, I met them in Mexico and rode back north with them. I have not committed any crime with Billy, sheriff. We parted at the border. That was some months ago. Billy said he was going back to Fort Sumner."

"Billy the Kid is dead. We don't know where Jose Chaves is."

Little Man Wolf stood quietly for a while.

"How, where?" he finally asked.

"Sheriff Pat Garrett cornered him in some bitch's house in Fort Sumner, and outshot him."

Little Man Wolf did not believe that Sheriff Pat Garrett could outshoot Billy the Kid. He had seen Billy draw and shoot. Billy had one characteristic that Little Man Wolf admired in the man: his deep loyalty to his friends. But, if that loyalty were not reciprocated, it could become a dangerous and tragic flaw. Garrett was not a true friend.

"I'm taking you in."

"What for?"

"We're checking all of Billy the Kid's friends. Men who rode with him in the Lincoln County War."

"Didn't even know him then."

"We'll see if there are any warrants against you."

"Can I make arrangements to have my horse and my dog fed and sheltered for the night?"

"Henry can take care of that for you."

"Be glad to."

"Easy now, boy"

"I was just going to get some money to give to Henry."

"No need for that. The town will take care of that. Just hand me your guns, your knife and your tomahawk slowly."

The following morning, the sheriff woke him up as he turned the key to the jail.

"Little Man Wolf, alias *Navajo Blanco*, alias Jeremiah McCall. According to this report, you killed an Ute Indian with a tomahawk when you were eight years old. At fourteen, you killed fifteen Mexican bandits. Then you killed Jesse Fremont and Tom Baxter at Betsy's Saloon when you where sixteen, as well as four bounty hunters."

"Two bounty hunters. Billy the Kid killed one; the dog killed the other one. I killed only two bounty hunters."

"Also at sixteen, you killed JB with a knife. Then at seventeen you killed six cowboys in Dodge City."

"I was a Deputy Marshal in Dodge City."

"There is a suspicion you killed Cherokee Lee near Juarez. Finally, Fred McAvoy. No arrests, no convictions, no warrants against you. How did you get away with all that?"

"I never draw first. Can I have my guns back?"

"Here. I don't want to see you here again Little Man Wolf."

"I didn't have the pleasure of knowing your name sheriff."

"The name is Sheriff Thomas Stanton."

Little Man Wolf was looking for Ken Stanton when he came to town. He was stopped from chasing him, and was put in jail by a sheriff named Stanton. Now it made sense.

"Remember, I said I don't want to see you in this town again."

"Oh, you will sheriff. The next time you see me I will be running for the sheriff's office against you."

He closed the door behind him, leaving Sheriff Stanton standing in the jail with an open mouth. He crossed the street and walked back to the saloon. People were following him with their eyes and whispering to each other. Five young boys were trailing him too close.

"That's Little Man Wolf, he's half Navajo," one boy was saying, proud about the knowledge he had on the man.

"Sheriff Stanton and three deputies arrested him last night, but they were so afraid of him they let him go before he got angry."

"Killed ten rustlers this side of the border, and fifteen Mexican bandits in Juarez."

"Killed Apaches, too."

"He is the fastest gun in the west, faster than anybody."

"Faster than Doc Holliday?"

"Faster."

"Faster than Wyatt Earp?"

"Faster."

"Faster that Johnny Ringo?"

"Faster."

"Faster than Billy the Kid?"

"I dunno. They're friends. Ain't they?"

Little Man Wolf stopped walking and said in a deep authoritative voice. "I heard you boys." Then he quickly turned around. The boys froze in horror, and then all ran away screaming. Even the adults around them were horrified. Little Man Wolf smiled and continued walking to the saloon.

"Good morning, Henry."

"Oh, good morning. You look well rested."

"Yep. Haven't had decent beds for my back in a while. The jail bunk, hard as it was, beats sleeping on pebbles and rocks. What do I owe you for my horse and my dog?"

"Not a thing. County paid for them. They're fed and rested too."

"Got any food?"

"I can whip up something for you."

"That would be great."

"Listen, I didn't get a chance to tell you last night that the man you were looking for, Ken, is the black sheep cousin of Sheriff Stanton."

"I figured that already. Maybe a brother, I thought."

"Sheriff's okay, he tries his best. But Johnny Ringo and Curly Bill Brosius and their hired fighting men run this whole area. They run it from Shakespeare, the town three miles south of here."

"Little Man Wolf!" somebody was calling outside.

"Who might that be?" Little Man Wolf asked.

"That could be the punk Billy Claiborne. He is Johnny Ringo's lackey. He fancies himself a fast gun."

"Little Man Wolf!" The voice was becoming louder and challenging.

"I think I heard his name before."

"Last October. The gunfight at the O.K. Corral in Tombstone, between the Earps, Doc Holiday, and the Clantons and McLaurys. Claiborne was there with the Clantons. He ran away. At the inquest, he said he wasn't armed."

"Now, he is out to prove something."

"He's been bullying anybody who would look sideways at him. That boy does not know any better."

"Let me see what he wants. How are you doing with the breakfast?"

"It'll be ready for you when you come back."

"Good."

Little Man Wolf looked out through the window first to see how many men were waiting for him outside. Lhachaeh was not around to watch his back, so he had to be extra careful. There was just this young man in the middle of street, in a fancy get up and a brand new holster with two six-shooters. Little Man Wolf went out and stood there at the boardwalk. He couldn't help smiling at the sight of the young man.

"Johnny Ringo and Curly Bill Brosius are looking for you. I'm here to save them the trouble."

"Who are you?"

"I'm Billy the Kid."

"You're not Billy the Kid."

"I'm Billy the Kid."

"William Bonney—Billy the Kid—was my friend. I know what he looked like."

"We'll, he's dead now. I'm Billy Claiborne. I'm Billy the Kid."

"You can call yourself anything, but there is only one Billy the Kid."

"Call me Billy the Kid and I'll let you off easy."

"Boy, why don't you just go back to your bosses before you hurt yourself. Tell them I'll see them later when I feel like it. "

"I want to see how fast you are."

"And you got it all figured out. You standing there with your back to the sun, while the sun rays are hitting my eyes, blinding me."

"Are you afraid to draw?"

"I don't want to kill you boy. I have nothing against you. I only kill people who need killing."

Suddenly, Billy Claiborne made a move to draw. He had barely touched the handle of his guns when Little Man Wolf put four grazing shots on each side of the man, cutting both the holster and his pant belt. His pants and his guns simply dropped to the ground.

Lhachaeh immediately ran from the stable as soon as it heard gunshots. Then it took its position on the ground in front of Little Man Wolf. Running Wind was right behind Lhachaeh.

"I could have cut you down dead center with my eyes closed, just from the sound of your voice and the rustling of the wind around your body."

Billy Claiborne was too shocked to move right away. He stood there shaking with his pants down.

"Leave the guns on the ground and pull up your pants. There are ladies around. You can pick up the guns from Sheriff Stanton later."

There was a sudden burst of laughter from the crowd that had quietly gathered to watch the gunfight.

Billy Claiborne complied quietly. Tears started flowing down his face. Little Man Wolf saw this.

"I'm sorry I did this to you. Perhaps, killing you would have been the kinder thing to do."

Claiborne stood there with his head bowed, still shaking and unable to think what to do.

"Lhachaeh, bring the man his horse."

Lhachaeh pulled the reins of Billy Claiborne's horse, and brought the animal to him.

Billy rode quietly out of town, tears still flowing down his cheeks. He could hear people laughing all around him.

Little Man Wolf turned around and went back in.

"I'm sorry I took too long."

"Not at all. I was enjoying the show myself," Henry said.

Lhachaeh took Running Wind's reins and looped them around the post. Then it sat on its haunches by the doorway, guarding the guns in the dirt. When Sheriff Stanton came into view, Lhachaeh turned and went inside the saloon.

"Now, you really did it," Sheriff Stanton said showing the guns he picked up from the ground. "Ringo and Brosius will skin you alive and leave you dying in the sun. They'll shoot up the town too in the process. I want you out of here now."

"By the way, Sheriff, thanks for taking good care of my animal friends, feeding them and all. And thanks for telling Henry to cook this wonderful breakfast for me. You are good people."

"Out, right now."

"I'm ready. Thank you, Henry."

"You bet."

At the door, Little Man Wolf turned around and said, "Sheriff, you know I came for your cousin Ken."

Sheriff Stanton was taken aback by the honesty of the statement. Then, with a quivering voice, he said, "What has to be done has to be done, but not in my town."

CHAPTER XXIV

Galeyville was quiet. There were no people on the street, no one on the roofs, and dust was piling up on the boardwalk. Little Man Wolf rode slowly, checking the windows for any unusual movements. The post office sign was falling down as it swayed in the wind. Businesses were closed and from all indications, the town was deserted. From some distance, he could hear the sound of iron being pounded on an anvil. He directed Running Wind toward the sound. It was a blacksmith working on some horseshoes.

"Good afternoon."

The blacksmith stopped working and eyed him curiously.

"Where is everybody?"

"Gone."

"Where to?"

"Heaven knows. This town is dead mister."

"What happened?"

"Lots of things. To start with, the silver mines around here had been failing. The smelter was moved to another town. They closed the post office. The stagecoach did its last run a week ago. To make it worse the Ringo and Brosius gang had been terrorizing the whole town. The good folks moved away."

"I'm looking for a fellow named Ken Stanton."

"Last April the Chiracahua Apache attacked the Ayers mining camp killing all thirty-five miners. They came up from the

Guadalupe Canyon in the Sonoran Mountains. Chiracahua Chief Nana, Geronimo, and Lozen have been roaming the hills."

"Lozen?"

"The sister of Chief Victorio."

"She wasn't killed then."

"They appear almost anywhere. General Crook has sent out Buffalo soldiers looking for them. You know, the Negro soldiers in blue uniform. They're good fighters and the Apache are afraid of them. But, that wily seventy-year-old Chief Nana is smarter than all of them. They've trapped him and Lozen so many times, but they always slip away. They're up there somewhere in those damned hills."

"Ken Stanton. Have you seen him?"

"Sure, I seen that troublemaker. Came two days ago looking for his friends. Had some horseshoes done. Said he came to see Brosius. He was in mighty hurry. You after him?"

"Maybe."

"You're Little Man Wolf, ain't you? I heard about you."

"Where is Brosius and his gang now? I see nobody around."

"Haven't you heard? Wyatt Earp, Doc Holliday and a posse of lawmen are looking for them for the murder of Morgan Earp and the shooting of Virgil. They all went into hiding. Some went to New Mexico, California, Colorado and Texas. I heard Johnny Ringo just came back to Charleston from Mexico, and is on his way here. I'm sure he'll skip Tombstone. Probably skirt around the mountains. Curly Bill Brosius is still holed up somewhere just north of town with some of his boys."

"How many with him?"

"Six or seven. Maybe eight. Don't rightly know."

"That horseshoe you're working on. Who is that for?"

"Nobody. Just need to keep working. Can't seem to tear myself away from this place."

Little Man Wolf looked at the blacksmith for a while. The man looked lost.

"Thanks for your help mister, and good luck."

"Yep, I should be packing soon. Got to make a new start. Maybe Lordsburg. Stagecoach is still running there."

Little Man Wolf turned Running Wind and rode slowly toward the north end of town.

"Lhachaeh. Go ahead. See what's out there. Be careful."

Lhachaeh started walking on the boardwalk, stopping once in a while to listen to any sound around him. As Lhachaeh turned a corner two shots rang out.

"God, you're a lousy shot! Didn't even nick that old wolf."

"You bumped into my arm, you idiot!"

"Sure, I did."

Lhachaeh had run back around the corner. Little Man Wolf got off Running Wind. He walked to the middle of the street. When the two men looked up from checking their guns, Little Man Wolf was already standing there facing them.

"I heard Ringo and Brosius are looking for me."

"Who are you, boy?"

Little Man Wolf said nothing.

"I said who are you?"

Little Man Wolf just stood there.

"Hey, that's the man Ken Stanton came to warn us about."

With the last word, the two men pointed their guns at Little Man Wolf. They were dead before they could even cock the hammer. The sounds of the shots brought Curly Bill Brosius and six men running out into the street with guns drawn. Little Man Wolf had run into an alley, and went around back of the buildings.

"These guys are dead!"

"Who saw what happened?" Brosius asked. "Was it Wyatt Earp?"

"If it was Earp there would be a whole posse down on us by now."

"It could be just one man."

"Ken—didn't you say this Little Man Wolf was after you?"

"The guy who killed Jesse and Tom at Betsy's Saloon?"

"Yeah. Billy Claiborne had a run in with him at Lordsburg. I couldn't quite make out what Billy was saying. He kept mumbling something, and then he ran off saying he was going to tell Johnny Ringo."

"That sonafabitch Little Man Wolf! I said I'll kill him when I see him," Curly Bill Brosius said. "He probably shot Jesse in the back. How else could he beat him?"

There was the sound of a pail being kicked in the back of a building. Three men ran toward the sound.

"Spread around boys."

"It's just a horse. It's a pinto. Looks like an Injun horse."

"It's Apache!"

"That is his horse, stupid. Little Man Wolf is a Navajo half breed."

"I heard he's a short man. About half your size."

"Don't let that fool you. His gun is as big as yours."

"It's actually bigger," a deep strong voice said from behind them.

The three men turned around. Little Man Wolf was standing there, holding a sawed-off shotgun. In an instant, the shotgun blasted the three men off their feet throwing them ten feet back. Then Little Man Wolf holstered the shotgun to his back.

"Where are the rest of them, Lhachaeh?"

Lhachaeh walked toward a run down saloon in the middle of the block.

"The blacksmith said maybe eight. That leaves three, and Brosius. There will be a shooter at the top of the stairs, one behind the bar, possibly with a shotgun, and one behind the back door. Brosius will be sitting at the table by the wall. His hands will be on the table, but his gun is on his lap covered with his hat. I guess we got that figured out."

Little Man Wolf was talking aloud to Lhachaeh who seemed to agree.

When they reached the saloon, Lhachaeh entered first with its head down and its eyes moving about to see if anyone was about to make a move.

"Come in Little Man Wolf, nobody is going to hurt you." It was a woman's voice. There was no response from outside.

"Come in, I say. Where the hell is he?"

"I'm here," Little Man Wolf said from the back of the room.

Everybody turned to look where the voice came from. They had expected him to swagger through the front door. Instead, Little Man Wolf had surprised Ken Stanton who was waiting behind the back door. He pushed him into the middle of the room.

"You forgot to take my gun," Stanton said, amused.

"I don't want to stop you from using it. I don't kill unarmed men."

"You have a lot of confidence, son," Curly Bill Brosius said.

"I heard you and Johnny Ringo are looking for me. What's it about?"

"We just want to talk to you."

Little Man Wolf could hear a shooter directly above him as the man shifted his weight to his other foot.

"I have no quarrel with you or Ringo, I just want this man."

"You killed two of our closest friends."

"I don't kill anybody who does not need killing."

"You shot Jesse in the back."

"I never shoot anybody in the back."

"How else can you kill him? He was one of the fastest gunfighters I've seen."

"Not fast enough."

"How d'ya know that?"

"Because he's dead."

There was a long silence. Suddenly, the man at the bar took out his shotgun. Little Man Wolf killed him before he could raise the gun above the counter. At the same time he shot the man upstairs through floor, and the man fell down on the table in front of him. Ken Stanton had his gun drawn but was unable to shoot because Lhachaeh got him by the wrist. Little Man Wolf cut him down. Brosius had drawn his gun at the same time as his men. Little Man

Wolf would have hit him dead center, but ended up just nicking him because the woman had also drawn a gun and shot at Little Man Wolf. He had to kill the woman. He never expected a shooter to be a woman. Brosius ran to the office and out the other door. By the time Little Man Wolf reached the office, he heard a horse galloping away.

Running Wind was already in the front of the saloon when Little Man Wolf came out. Brosius was riding south. He was gone from sight quickly, hidden by the hillocks that surrounded Galeyville. Little Man Wolf followed the tracks for days. He had to end this problem now, or it would rear its head again when he least expected it.

The tracks lead toward Iron Springs waterhole. Little Man Wolf got off Running Wind. This would be a good place for Curly Bill Brosius to lie in ambush. A few yards away from the waterhole, a shot from a 12-guage shotgun rang out. This was followed by two shots from a six-shooter. The shots were not directed at Little Man Wolf. Cautiously, he approached the waterhole. A man in a dark suit was standing there over the body of Curly Bill Brosius.

"Is that you Wyatt?"

"Who calls?"

"Little Man Wolf."

"I thought you'd be around soon. Come on down. It's okay, Doc. It's Little Man Wolf."

"Well, I'll be. What are you doing here, Little Man Wolf?" Doc Holliday asked.

"I was tracking Brosius from Galeyville."

"We were tracking Johnny Ringo from Charleston. He was headed here to Galeyville."

"Then the matter is now closed," Little Man Wolf said.

"Not quite. There is still this business with Ringo," Wyatt Earp said.

"I understand."

"Where are you going now?"

"I will be riding north."

"The old McCall farm near Prescott?"

Little Man Wolf nodded.

"Visit my folks' gravesite."

"Say a prayer in my name, too, Either One."

Little Man Wolf smiled.

"I will. I'll tell them you said hello."

"Well, then I'll see you around," Wyatt Earp said. "You too, Lhachaeh."

Lhachaeh wiggled its tail.

"You bet," Little Man Wolf said, nodding to Doc Holliday at the same time.

Running Wind walked over and sat on the ground. Little Man Wolf got on its back. It stood up, turned north and slowly walked away with Lhachaeh at its side. Then the walk became a trot. Then a gallop. Faster and faster until they were racing, and finally they disappeared from view in the steamy haze of the afternoon sun.

"There goes the fastest gun I've ever seen," Doc Holliday said.

"Yep," Wyatt Earp agreed.

In West Turkey Creek Canyon there stood an unusual creation of nature. Three trees had grown and fused together around an eighteen-inch boulder, forming a natural recessed seat. A man that had been dead no more than a day was found seated in there. On his right side leaned a Winchester rifle. His right hand held a Colt .45, with one shell fired. There was one bullet hole in his head, just above the ear. His head was partially scalped. The dead man was identified as Johnny Ringo.

EPILOGUE

Little Man Wolf returned to the farm where, as a child, he was Jeremiah McCall. Silently, he said a Christian prayer for the souls of his departed parents. Then, he placed the scalp of Laughing Deer on top of a cord of cedar wood in the burnt remains of their hogan. He surrounded it with sacred ornaments of white shell, blue turquoise stone, yellow abalone shell, and jet-black stone. He lit the wood into a fire, and watched the fragrant smoke spiral up higher and higher, reaching into the sky until it disappeared among the clouds. Then, he knelt down and sang the Night Way songs for the safe journey of their spirits into the next world. At dawn, he rode back to Diné Land, where the First Woman placed the Navajo people between the four magnificent, sacred mountains. There he would be with Little Sunflower, at peace and balanced once more with Mother Earth and Father Sky, and all the spirits of the land.